'*I have a great desire to carry you away with me,*' Sir Richard Calder tells Lady Alicia Bartolf. But what hope has she of marriage to a man who wears the white rose of her family's Yorkist enemies?

Seizing her opportunity to flee, Alicia presents herself at Leet Castle—only to find that Sir Richard is no longer so welcoming . . .

Who is the mysterious Lady Elizabeth who receives all his attention? Had Alicia been foolish to believe that he would marry her? To cast herself so recklessly on the mercy of this intriguing enemy?

LORD OF LEET CASTLE

OLGA DANIELS

MILLS & BOON LIMITED
London · Sydney · Toronto

First published in Great Britain 1984
by Mills & Boon Limited, 15–16 Brook's Mews,
London W1A 1DR

ISBN 0 263 74704 2

Set in 11 on 11½pt Linotron Times
05-0684-58,000

Photoset by Rowland Phototypesetting Ltd
Bury St Edmunds, Suffolk
Made and printed in Great Britain by
Cox and Wyman Ltd, Reading

CHAPTER
ONE

Greensleeves was all my joy,
  Greensleeves was my delight,
Greensleeves was my heart of gold,
  And who but my Lady Greensleeves?

THE VOICE, sweet and young, trilled through the spring woodland which bordered the road to the castle. The unexpected sound caught the attention of the man who stood close to a large oak tree, pressed with his back to its trunk, camouflaged in his dark brown cloak. He had been watching the track below but now, with no pleasure in his expression, he turned and sought for a glimpse of the singer.

She was slight of figure, moving with a springing step that matched the lightness of her voice, holding in her hand a posy of primroses. He could see little of her face, sheltered as it was by the forward fall of the hood above her cape, but she held her long full skirts in one hand, lifting them clear of the vegetation, revealing ankles, neat even though covered by woollen stockings, her feet encased in thick leather pattens. She had not seen him and, as he watched her for a few moments, the picture she presented of youthful simplicity caused the impatience he felt to soften a little.

Then more distantly than the girl's singing, the

jangle of harness and the clip-clop of horse's hooves jarred into his ears, bringing him back to the purpose of his mission. He scanned the dusty road below and as it rounded a bend, perhaps a quarter of a mile away, the first of the horsemen came in sight. They would pass within a few feet of him and he had no desire to be seen. The wench, singing so blithely, would be almost certain to attract their attention, would cause them to peer into the depths of the wood—and certainly then he, too, would be discovered. She seemed to be quite lost in the carefree enjoyment of her song and of her surroundings, bending to examine a plant which grew at the foot of some hazel saplings, then moving on again until she was only a few feet from where he stood. If she had heard the approaching horsemen she ignored them. With a quick movement he leapt towards her.

Lady Alicia was taken completely by surprise as she was flung to the ground. The man seemed enormous as she looked up, and in that instant before his arms closed around her she had a glimpse of dark tousled hair, of a thick woollen cloak. She had no time to cry out, the song changed to a sharp note of surprise and then her mouth was covered by a strong masculine hand. He held her down on the mossy earth.

She was terrified. Horrible tales of robbers and cut-throats who roamed the forests flashed through her mind. She had never dreamed that such men would venture so close to the castle, the day had been so beautiful, no inkling of danger had come to her—what would he do? She had no jewels or gold on her person to give him—she had dressed as a peasant, he must have seen that. Would he try to rape her? She almost fainted at the thought—she tried to struggle, to free herself from his grasp, but his grip on her only tightened.

'Lie still, little maid, and I'll not hurt you,' he whispered.

His voice had an edge of steel that warned her that resistance would be futile. She felt weak and helpless, his body pressed down on hers, his hand still covered her mouth, she dared not move. She had been brought up like all children in the late fifteenth century, especially girls, to obey the commands of the males of the household. Any misdemeanour was punished with a beating, so she knew all too well their superior strength and how it could, and often was, employed unmercifully to achieve obedience.

She lay still, only her wide open eyes trying to assess this frightening situation, her heart beating so fast she was sure it would choke her, the weight of his body was still atop hers, crushing her to the ground, and the smell of the dank leaves and the brilliant green mosses was earthy but by no means unpleasant to her.

Strangely, though he had used such force to bring her down and hold her close, he had not hurt her and, though there was some discomfort in this undignified posture in which he held her, she felt no pain. Even the hand which continued to press upon her mouth was not entirely unpleasant, its fingers clean, a trifle salty. She stared up at him, but he was not regarding her, he craned his head, looking in the direction of the road, and then she heard for the first time the clatter of the horses' hooves, the jangle of the harness, the mutter of men's voices and, though she could not see them, she guessed a

large troop of horsemen was passing by. She was
not surprised by the sound; she had known they
were expected at the castle, but there seemed to be
a much larger number than she would have expected.

She wriggled, she wished she could see them, but
her movement brought a sharp response from her
captor, who instantly applied just a little more
pressure, enough for her to realise that if she really
struggled he would not hesitate to use more force.
She had to lie still, fuming, biding her time till he
should relax his grip one little bit. The hard jawline
of the man's face jutted out above her. His skin was
tanned, as that of one who spends much time out of
doors, his profile etched hawk-like, strong but fine,
but his mouth held a sensitivity that made her less
afraid of him, though his eyes were hidden so that
she could not look into them.

Obviously there was a purpose in his assessment
of the passing horsemen; it must be important to
him to know their strength, their numbers, their
armoury. Was he simply some brigand who roamed
the woods, robbing and attacking travellers when
he could? If so, he was wise to stay hidden from such
numbers—they could have flushed him out and
taken him captive in a matter of minutes. Yet somehow she could not believe he was simply a ruffian
—his hair, for one thing, had been cut neatly to just
above his shoulders, it curled and had a clean shine.

She could guess who the horsemen were and
wished she could observe them herself, especially
Sir Hobart Kimball, who would ride at their head.
For several days now there had been talk of the
arrival of this man—and part of that talk had been
that she, Lady Alicia Bartolf, should be wed to him

ere the summer departed. She had had no say in such plans as she was merely a chattel, living with her uncle, Rufus Blount, who had moved into Braister Castle some five years previously after her father and mother had died of the pestilence.

For several minutes the air was filled with the sound of the men and horses passing in leisurely fashion on this the last stage of their journey to the castle. Then gradually the clatter receded into the distance and, as they disappeared entirely, the man relaxed his hold on Alicia.

Immediately she began to struggle; she kicked and he leapt away rather smartly, jumping to his feet and looking down at her with a laugh on his face. Then she realised that her skirts had become tumbled, lifted almost to her knees. It infuriated her even more to realise that this ruffian—she was determined to think of him as such—was regarding her legs so indecorously revealed. Nor had she entirely dismissed the fear of rape from her mind. Hastily she pulled down her skirts and tried to get up into a more dignified position, all in one movement which rendered her so unsteady that she almost fell back to the ground. Then his hands caught her arms and she was assisted gently up until she was standing face to face with him.

He raised his hand and pushed back the hood which covered her hair and forehead so that he could see her face, and a smile lifted the corners of his mouth, a conspiratorial smile as if they shared some secret.

'My thanks, sweet maid. I am grateful for your co-operation in remaining still.'

'I had little chance to do otherwise,' Alicia replied tartly.

He chuckled. 'True, but I must say I have never before floored so delightful an opponent. If opponents we have to be?'

'Take your hands off me at once—or I'll scream—'

Before she could put her threat into operation, his arms closed around her tighter again and he kissed her. His lips were as strong and possessive as his arms had been when he held her. It was an unhurried kiss, his mouth having sought hers was in no hurry to leave it, and momentarily she was so astonished that she stood with the whole of her body pressed close to his, enveloped within his arms and his thick cloak. Never before had she been kissed by any man other than a relation—and it was many years since she had experienced even that. This was entirely different and it shocked her to realise that she found it pleasant—and that reaction made her even angrier.

She was about to start struggling and kicking again, but before she could do so he released his hold and took a step back.

'How dare you manhandle me so—you—you brigand!'

'Methinks you are more agreeable when you have silence forced upon you.'

'You shall be punished for this—I could scream—and call out the castle guards.'

He raised his eyebrows and regarded her speculatively, as if weighing up her words.

'Then scream—though I assure you you have nothing more to fear from me. And long before the guards could get here I should have disappeared into the greenwood.'

'You may scoff. I assure you it would go ill with

you, if you were discovered here molesting me.'

At last her words seemed to have some effect upon him. He regarded her thoughtfully, and something in his expression, in the handsome lines of his clean-shaven face, made her quite sure that he was no ordinary brigand. Perhaps he had once been a gentleman and had fought on the wrong side in this terrible civil conflict they called the War of the Roses. It was now three years since the Earl of Warwick had, in the spring of 1461, presented the young Earl of March, son of the late Duke of York, to a great assembly of Londoners in St John's Field, Clerkenwell. There he had challenged the people whether they thought Henry was worthy to reign as their king.

'Nay! Nay!' had come the great response.

'Then will you take the Earl of March for your king?' Warwick had cried.

'Yea! Yea!'

A few days later he had walked to Westminster Abbey to receive the sceptre and be declared King Edward IV. He was not quite nineteen years old.

Alicia had heard of the scene many times and although her uncle was one of those who had supported Lancaster, King Henry and the red rose, he had refrained from becoming actively involved. Holding on to—or even increasing—his possessions was more important to him. Many who had loyally fought for Henry before he had been forced to flee to France with his French wife, Margaret, had lost property and fortune. Was this such a man, she wondered? His voice cut into her thoughts.

'Who are you?'

'I am Lady Alicia Bartolf,' she replied, lifting her head haughtily.

She expected him to make some obeisance, to acknowledge her superior status, as was customary, but he merely threw back his head and laughed.

'In that case, how is it that you are roaming in the woods unattended?'

She stamped her foot, angry that he should doubt her word, although it was a sensible enough question. She held her head high, allowing him to see by her demeanour that she was no common peasant girl—then at last he seemed able to acknowledge the truth of her statement. He placed one foot delicately in front of the other, made a sweeping gesture with his arm and bowed with natural grace. Yet there was still a twinkle in his eyes that made her own sense of humour return to her, and she softened enough to give him the explanation he sought.

'It was such a delightful day—the drawbridge has been lowered all morning, for the villagers and traders have been in and out in vast numbers, bringing things for the feast in honour of Sir Hobart,' she said. 'Finally a whole flock of geese were brought in and some of them escaped and there was such an uproar, with everyone chasing them in all directions, so I slipped out without anyone seeing me. Now I must get back, for I've tarried here much longer than I intended.'

Indeed, even as she spoke she turned and began to run down to the road. She would be punished severely if she were discovered outside the precincts of the castle, but the woods had beckoned her irresistibly with their beauty. The rebellious streak that she had inherited from her father had led her into trouble more than once before.

'Farewell, Lady Alicia,' the stranger called after her.

She did not reply but hurried on until she reached the dusty track. Then she turned and saw that the stranger was still watching her from the shadow of the trees, but when she glanced back again a few moments later, he had gone.

The circular tower rose high, dominating the flat countryside with its pinkish-grey bricks, its windows catching the rosy glint of the lowering sun. Within its walls and moat there were several acres of courtyard and buildings, space easily to accommodate in rough comfort the troops and horses of Sir Hobart, as well as the many servants and guards that were normally there.

Alicia began to panic in case the drawbridge should have been raised by now, making it impossible for her to return as unnoticed as she had left. Her escape had been so impetuous that she had pushed this difficulty out of her mind, but now it had to be faced. She trembled as she thought what punishment might be meted out to her should her escapade ever reach the ears of either her uncle or her aunt.

She breathed a sigh of relief as she came within sight of the gatehouse with its tall towers, and realised that the drawbridge was still down. Within the courtyard there was great movement and bustle as the needs of troops and horses were attended to. Alicia approached cautiously, pulled her hood down so that it covered most of her face, and resolutely walked across. Immediately one of the guards stepped forward ready to challenge her right of entry.

'Halt,' he commanded.

Alicia glanced around apprehensively. Neither her uncle nor her aunt were in the vicinity, so she lifted the hood so that the guard could see her face.

'Do you not know who I am?' She spoke imperiously.

The man's jaw dropped in surprise. 'Aye, my lady—but—but where have you come from?'

'How dare you question me? My uncle would not be pleased to know that you had so far neglected your duty as to be unaware that I had been out. I've a good mind to report you to the captain.'

'No need to do that, if you please, my lady.' He looked scared.

'I shall say nothing on this occasion—and I advise you not to mention it to anyone either.'

'No, my lady. I certainly shall say nothing. Thank you, my lady.'

Another man came to the door of the guardroom and Alicia pulled her hood forward and hurried on. She did not make straight for the main entrance to the castle, but walked round the side of the great edifice. She was safely back, but there could still be awkward questions if she were seen to be outside the confines of those areas normally frequented by the ladies.

Presently she came to the formal gardens, edged with low boxwood hedges, each of which contained a segment of a circle with grass paths and crescent shapes filled with flowers completing the geometric layout. In the centre was a circular pool. It would have been an attractive place to saunter on such a pleasantly sunny day, and Alicia slowed her footsteps.

She was minded to linger there and day-dream for a time—to turn over in her mind that extraordinary adventure which had befallen her. Who was this stranger? She wished that she had asked him for his name—but why? She would surely never see him again, and that thought brought with it a strange feeling of sadness.

'Alicia—come here at once.'

It was Aunt Margaret's voice, shrilling from where she stood at the side doorway.

'Where have you been, you thoughtless wench? Did you not know that Sir Hobart was due to arrive this day?'

Obediently Alicia hurried up the steps to where her aunt waited, her stern old face nipped in anger, as was the case so often that she was scarcely ever seen to be relaxed and happy.

'I apologise, my good aunt,' said Alicia, breathless from her haste. 'Has my lord arrived then?'

'He has indeed and you must away to your chamber immediately and prepare for such time as he may ask to see you. Whatever do you look like? Anyone would think you were a simple peasant— pray keep out of his sight until you have made yourself decent to adorn the household of a knight.'

Alicia dropped a quick curtsy as she came up close to her aunt on the top step.

'Aunt Margaret—you have seen him?'

'Of course.'

'What manner of man is he?'

'What foolish questions are these? He is suitable, he has land and position—that is all that matters.'

'But—'

'Get away, up the back stairs to your room.'

Aunt Margaret delivered a strong push that Alicia, having expected it, was able to dodge so that it only partly made contact. She needed no further bidding to run, her pattens clattering on the stone stairs as if the devil himself were after her. She counted herself lucky to have returned to the castle with no hint that she had been so far afield, and with no more admonishment than that angry shove from her aunt. Blows, cuffs or whipping were the usual order of the day from those in authority to any menial beings, servants, children or even wives for that matter. Alicia's position in the household was of even less account than that of a daughter would have been, for she was only the ward of Rufus Blount and he made no secret of his intention of making a match for her that would be advantageous to him at the earliest opportunity.

Even when she was married she would merely transfer this subservience from her uncle to her husband, and she could only hope and pray that this nobleman her uncle had chosen for that role would look kindly on her, that she could be pleasing to him and that he would treat her gently when they were wed. If indeed they were married—first there was this hurdle of meeting him and of presenting herself as well as possible so that he might find no fault in her. Alicia, at eighteen, was of an age to be married and since both her uncle and her aunt seemed to delight in making her life at the castle unpleasant, she had decided that she would welcome the release which marriage would give her.

It was but the exchange of one form of bondage for another—but perhaps, in time, if she proved to be a good and loyal wife, she would win her lord's esteem, so that he would treat her with respect and consideration. Indeed, although her uncle obviously had the right to beat his wife, Alicia could never remember such a thing happening. So it was that she was able to look forward to marriage as a release from the trials that constantly bedevilled her life.

She hurried along to the chamber where she slept and there Jenny, her maid, was waiting and her obvious anxiety changed to relief when Alicia rushed in. She had carried up a ewer of hot water which was now merely warm, and had placed the pewter bowl in readiness on the chest which doubled as a washstand. The walls were hung with rich tapestries and the boarded floor was strewn with rushes which were soft and warm. Bunches of lavender and rosemary hung by the bed to keep the air sweet-smelling. There was one small arched window with leaded lights.

'Hurry, my lady,' urged Jenny, taking the cloak which Alicia shrugged from her shoulders. 'Mistress Margaret has been on the rampage because you were not here to greet Sir Hobart.'

'I imagine I shall meet him soon enough,' said Alicia. 'It was so beautiful in the woods this afternoon.'

She could not have told that to anyone else, but Jenny was her friend, as well as her maid.

'Oh, my lady—you surely haven't been out in the woods? You might have been lost,' cried Jenny.

With a merry laugh Alicia told how she had escaped over the drawbridge when the geese had caused the uproar in the courtyard. She made the story so funny that Jenny could not help laughing too, but at the same time she continued to urge her young mistress to hurry, helped her to take off her everyday garments and then poured the warm water into the bowl.

'Them woods is full of danger—I wouldn't dare go into them myself. Never know who you might meet,' Jenny muttered.

Alicia smiled, and a flush stole over her cheeks as she remembered the strong arms of the stranger and how they had closed so tightly around her, pulling her to the ground. The feel of the kiss that he had bestowed on her seemed almost to have bruised her mouth—never before had a man kissed her so. It seemed to Alicia that her lips must show some sign and she touched them with cool fingers; as she did so, the odour of the mosses from the ground where she had lain added to the pleasantness of the sensation. Her day-dream was broken as Jenny chattered on.

'Such a to-do there's been, with my lord Hobart arriving earlier than was expected and Mistress Margaret frantic to know where you were. She blamed me for not keeping with you—'

'I'm sorry, Jenny. I had no idea I should be so late. I—I shouldn't have lingered so. But I'm here now—help me to get ready.'

She soaped her hands and standing naked washed herself thoroughly, while Jenny began towelling her dry almost before she had finished. Alicia's best gown was laid out on the bed in readiness and very quickly Jenny helped her to step into the under-dress, the *cotte*, which was a delicate shade of blue. Over this went the gown of golden colour, richly embroidered, trimmed with ermine fur at the hem and round the neckline. There it was cut so low it dipped to the waist, revealing the top of the *cotte* above her delicately rounded breasts. The sleeves were long and close fitting, trimmed at the cuffs with ermine, and a wide belt drew the garments tight so that her slender figure was shown to best advantage.

The dressing of Alicia's hair took a considerable time and could not be hurried. She sat on a stool while Jenny brushed the long blonde tresses and braided them and fastened the plaits close to her head. Over this was wound a length of cloth, covering the hair tightly and holding a frame over which the butterfly headdress of starched muslin was carefully draped. To complete her toilette a fine chain of gold with a bright enamelled medallion was fastened around her neck. Jenny stood back to check that all was in order, and a satisfied smile lifted the corners of her mouth. She was a country girl, of about the same age as Alicia and completely devoted to her young mistress.

'You look beautiful, my lady. My lord Hobart will be enchanted when he sees you.'

Alicia was suddenly fearful. 'Have you seen him, Jenny?'

Jenny moved away and began to busy herself with pouring the water from the bowl into a pail to be carried downstairs and emptied into the moat. Alicia's heart sank.

'What did he look like?'

'That's not for me to say, my lady,' Jenny answered, and her lips closed tight.

Her expression was revealing enough. She had obviously had a glimpse of the knight and her reluctance to talk suggested that she had not liked what she had seen. But there was no chance for Alicia to press further on the subject, for her aunt came into the chamber at that moment. Her eyes darted over Alicia. There was no love in them, no admiration, only a cool assessment of her as a chattel that was about to be bartered on the marriage market.

'Put this on.'

She handed a necklace to Jenny. 'That thing is not rich enough for tonight.'

The stones set in the fine gold chain glittered so brightly they could only be diamonds. Alicia had a sudden remembrance that she had seen them before.

'It's my mother's necklace!' she exclaimed.

'It was,' corrected her aunt. 'But you may wear it for tonight. And be sure to be on your best behaviour, my girl, or you'll suffer for it tomorrow.'

'Yes, Aunt Margaret.'

She stood meekly as her aunt pulled and prodded at one or two points in her garments, twitching the headgear into position regardless of whether her fingers hurt. The little adjustments were not even necessary, it was simply that Aunt Margaret could not help her desire to hurt, almost as if she would have preferred to administer a sharp slap and only desisted with an effort.

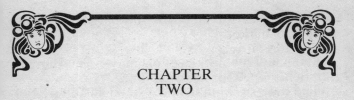

CHAPTER
TWO

THE SCENE in the great hall was full of colour, bustle, excitement, chatter and the smells of ale mulling, of pork roasting on the spit over the fire with lard spluttering down into the ashes. Every candle in the two great chandeliers overhead had been lit, and others on the long trestle tables glittered on the silverware, the pewter had been burnished till it shone and piles of bread, fruit and pickles had already been placed there in preparation for the feast which would soon be served.

The clothes of the men were gay and almost garish. Some wore long gowns with wide sleeves so long that they touched the ground, others had short tunics edged with fur in shades of red, blue or yellow and hose of equally gay colours that showed off their legs. Their feet were thrust into long narrow shoes with pointed toes. The tapestries on the walls of the huge room had threads of gold which were picked up by the glow of the blazing log fire, though the rest of their delicate embroidery was lost in the dimness.

Alicia looked around anxiously. Uncle Rufus was there, standing commandingly with his great bulk back to the fire, waving a silver mug of ale in his hand as he emphasised a point he was making to the ugly old man who sat, legs outstretched before him, leaning back on a bench surrounded by cushions. He was dark-faced, and wore a little round red and gold hat from which a few straggling strands of dark, greasy hair hung down to the fur collar of his tunic. His nose was bulbous and he was supping at a mug of ale, careless of whether he spilled it down his clothes. Alicia's heart sank. She would have found it impossible to proceed towards him across the floor had it not been for the tight impelling grip of her aunt's hand on her arm.

There was no escape, forward she had to go, and instinctively her eyes dropped to the floor not from simple modesty, but to conceal the shock and horror that had sprung into her breast. Surely they couldn't—they wouldn't—compel her to marry such a man as this?

When she looked up again, it was at her uncle's face, but there was no comfort to be read into what she saw there. He was beaming, looking well pleased with himself, nodding with approval at her appearance.

'There, my dear Hobart—what do you think of her? As fine a wench as you'll find anywhere in Norfolk, eh?'

Her eyes widened with terror. Beseechingly she stared at her uncle. He only laughed at her, gave her a shove in the direction of the old man on the bench.

'Don't look at me, Alicia, look at this fine gentleman. He's a great knight, is Sir Hobart Kimball, and he's likely to do you the honour of asking for your hand in marriage.'

'Curtsy, Alicia,' Aunt Margaret hissed in her ear, at the same time giving her arm a pinch. 'Remember to behave yourself, or you'll account for it to me tomorrow.'

There was nothing for it but to obey. Meekly Alicia took hold of her full skirts and dropped a low obeisance in the direction of Sir Hobart. As she rose to her feet again she was staring him straight in the face, and this time it was the deep scar across his forehead that caught her attention. It had healed with a nasty puckering of the skin that pulled his eye down towards his sunken cheek. It made it impossible to read anything of his thoughts, of his character. She tried to tell herself that beneath this ugly exterior might be hidden a kindly heart, but somehow it was impossible to believe that.

Sir Hobart took another swig at his mug of ale and rubbed the froth from his mouth with the back of his hand. Alicia could not tell whether he found the sight of her pleasing or not; there was no alteration in his expression as he gazed at her. It almost seemed to be a matter of indifference to him what she looked like, nevertheless he took his time in assessing her.

'Not much meat on her, is there?'

'She's young yet, still time to grow. Besides I'll wager you'd soon be able to fatten her out, eh Hobart?' Uncle Rufus said coarsely.

It was a mark in Sir Hobart's favour that he did not respond to the vulgar joke, but it appeared to be more from a taciturn nature than from any sensitivity to Alicia's feelings.

'I like a woman with a bit more meat on her,' he said.

Alicia's heart stilled slightly. Perhaps he would take such a dislike to her slightness of figure that he would not press for her hand. Her hope was quickly dispelled.

'She's a good-tempered, amenable wench,'

Uncle Rufus declared. 'Won't cause any trouble.'

Sir Hobart lifted his hand dismissively. 'The wench doesn't live who can get the better of me, Rufus. I have no fears—be she ever so headstrong, I reckon I could soon tame her.'

He put his hand to the small whip that he carried at his belt and, as though to demonstrate his meaning even more clearly, pulled it out and flicked it across the shoulders of the servant who stood behind the bench. The youth side-stepped and avoided the full sting of the swipe, but it demonstrated clearly enough the relationship that existed between master and servant. Alicia flinched—and this time Sir Hobart allowed himself a cruel laugh, for he had kept his eyes firmly fixed on her the while.

'I stand for no trouble from my subordinates—but you attend to me like a good and faithful wife and you'll have nothing to fear.'

Uncle Rufus was overjoyed. 'You'll take her? The match is agreed?'

'Not so fast, Rufus. I haven't heard the lass speak yet—has she got a tongue.'

'Say something, you stupid girl. Don't just stand there like a dummy,' hissed Aunt Margaret.

She gave Alicia another shove, which precipitated her so close to Sir Hobart that she almost stumbled into his lap.

'Oh!' She gave a little scream, then instinctively began to apologise. 'I—I'm so sorry. I beg your pardon, sir.' Terror made the words tremble on her lips.

'The girl's overcome by the honour you may offer her,' said Aunt Margaret. 'But I can assure you she has been well taught in all those things that a good wife should know, she can read and write passably well and she can sew and run the household and ensure that the servants attend to their duties properly, and for your entertainment she can sing and dance. I've trained her myself and, I assure you, you'll not find a wench more fitted to be your wife than my niece here.'

'Then let her begin by fetching me a refill of this good ale,' said Sir Hobart, thrusting the mug into Alicia's hands.

She bobbed a little curtsy and, turning, held the mug out to the servant who was hovering close by with a frothing jug. It was the work of a moment to get it replenished.

'Now let us share a drink together. Take a sup, lass, before you hand it back to me,' commanded Sir Hobart.

Alicia had little liking for ale and still less to put her lips to the brim so recently touched by the moist, slobbery mouth of Sir Hobart, but she dared not refuse and delicately took the tiniest of sips. Her action brought a great bellow of laughter from him, and he slapped his great thigh as if he was mightily pleased.

'Ho-ho—she's a rare pernickity lass, this one. I reckon it could be mightily pleasant to train her to my ways. Come and sit down beside me. What did they say your name was?'

'Alicia, sire.'

'Alicia. Aye, it suits you.'

He took the mug from her and lifted it to down a great draught of ale, by which time Aunt Margaret had pushed Alicia down on to the bench beside him. She sat, stiffly upright, trying to prevent her body from making any contact with his, still half hoping that he would decide against the match. If he did, she knew she would have to endure a beating from her aunt tomorrow, but that seemed a lesser evil than the dread of being married to this man. He threw an arm around her waist and pulled her close to him but she turned her head away, looking desperately down towards where her hands were clasped so tightly in her lap that she could see the knuckles whitened. Sir Hobart did not press his advances.

'She's a coy one, but I'll warrant we'll have some merry times together. 'T'will brighten my household up to have a young wife about it again. It's more than a year since my last wife died and high time I took another. Aye, Rufus—I'm agreeable, so long as the dowry is right.'

'No doubt about that, Hobart. You already know what Alicia brings to you as her portion— indeed I have taken the liberty of instructing a lawyer to draw up the necessary documents so that the match can go ahead with all possible speed.'

'Good. Then let's to the table. I'll wager everybody's ready for their viands.'

A look of smug triumph passed swiftly between Aunt Margaret and Uncle Rufus at the successful outcome of their scheme. Alicia felt as if all life had been drained from her, her youthful dreams of a gallant lover were killed in that instant, she knew of no way of escape from this appalling fate. The beautiful butterfly headdress trembled around her pale face as she looked with wordless supplication from the face of her aunt to that of her uncle. They did not even glance in her direction. Aunt Margaret clapped her hands sharply and issued the orders that brought the servants scuttling to and fro to serve the meal which had been awaiting the command.

Sir Hobart Kimball was a rich catch as far as they were concerned; he had extensive lands and several properties and could therefore call to arms a good number of men if required. It was that which Rufus and Margaret cherished—not for Alicia's aggrandisement but as a connection which would enhance their own prestige, add to their power, ally them to those estates and allow them to call on the might of Sir Hobart in any scheme they had of increasing their own holdings of land. In those lawless times the seizing of property was often brought about by force which made influential friends of paramount importance. She wondered a little that Sir Hobart should have agreed to the match. It was not simply for lust, let alone for love, that he had agreed to the terms of the marriage contract. She had no real knowledge what had actually made him willing to wed her—only one thing was certain, the dowry which her uncle had dangled before Sir Hobart must have contained some item to tempt him, though he had always declared that Alicia had inherited nothing from her parents.

The training of years in obedience, in the subjugation of her own will, served to give her strength to hold her head proudly high as she walked towards the long table at the top of the room and took her place beside Sir Hobart. To have acted in any other way would have brought the wrath of Aunt Margaret upon her, and she had suffered from too many beatings in the past to risk yet another when there was no hope of escaping from this situation.

In came the steaming dishes, the venison, the

boar's head with an apple decoratively in its mouth, the capons, geese and the pigeon pies. The company fell to eating with greed and pleasure, but Alicia found her mouth dry, she was unable to do more than pick at the food.

'Eat up, girl—no wonder you're so thin,' complained Sir Hobart as he noticed her pingling beside him.

Alicia gave him a bleak smile and obediently put a small morsel into her mouth, but it was tasteless and tough and she found difficulty in swallowing. Fortunately Sir Hobart took little more heed of her, being more interested in what was on his own platter.

Vast quantities of food were consumed and gallons of ale and wine found their way down many receptive throats. At the tables were all the followers of Sir Hobart, a great company which he had brought with him to the castle, and in addition Rufus had invited many neighbouring influential landowners. Was it all in honour of the betrothal of herself to Sir Hobart, Alicia began to wonder? Or was there some other meaning behind the great concourse? Her thoughts strayed to that morning in the woods and to the man who had held her prisoner while he took note of the passing of the troop of men.

Those were wild and lawless days with civil war between the rival factions who followed either the red rose of Lancaster or the white rose of Yorkshire. Many ruffians roamed loose in the forests so that men did not travel alone, but the great company that Sir Hobart had brought with him—what was their purpose? She thought of asking him, but when she turned towards him he was tearing the flesh from a goose leg, the grease ran down his stubbly chin and revulsion made the question die on her lips.

He was horrible, rough, coarse, old—he must be be almost sixty, she guessed. She knew that he had been married twice before and both of his wives had died, the first in childbirth, when the infant had been stillborn. The other had been childless, dying after a long illness, so that there was no heir. There was little comfort in those stark facts and the knowledge added to the repugnance she felt for him. The scar on his face might have been gained honourably in battle, but it was a disfigurement it was difficult to ignore—though she felt she could have overlooked it on a younger, on a nicer man. She shivered at the recollection of the undeserved stinging with the whip he had bestowed on his servant, merely to show his power.

If only he had been like that stranger she had met that morning in the woods. Again she wondered—who was he? His garb had been that of a poor man, yet his manners were those of a gentleman—he had been clean, pleasant to look upon. Even the recollection of that kiss he had stolen from her brought a sweet sensation to her lips. If only she could marry a man such as he, she would gladly follow wherever he went and would never crave for riches, for power. Position and land meant nothing to her.

At last the meal was finished. The empty dishes were stacked up, piles of bones and scraps which would be given to the poor were carried out of the hall, the tables were cleared and the trestles dismantled to be stood by the walls so that a space was cleared for dancing and entertainment. In the gallery above the musicians struck up a merry jig and a group of travelling players came in, there were harlequins and jugglers, acrobats and a jester.

The company were in a good mood, all were replete and most had drunk so much wine and ale that even the smallest joke could set them laughing uproariously. Nevertheless Alicia glanced around her anxiously, as she knew from past experience that this state of euphoria could easily erupt into belligerence, that a man's pride when he was in his cups could easily be pricked and that it would take little to make a fight break out somewhere in the hall. After the strolling players had performed all that was in their repertoire, the musicians began to play again and this time it was a merry little tune, well known throughout Norfolk, which heralded a jolly longways dance.

After they had left the table Alicia had perforce to remain beside Sir Hobart. There had been no way of avoiding his company, for when she had attempted to stray from his side, her aunt had imperiously motioned her back. Now the old man heaved himself to his feet, clumsily because he had stiffened up a little with sitting and was also rather unsteady from the amount of alcohol he had consumed.

'Come, wench.' He grasped Alicia's hand. 'Let us tread a measure together.'

'Certainly, sire.'

He led her to where the couples were lining up for the dance and, as befitted his elevated station in life, took his place at the top of the set. The musicians played a chord to signal they were about to begin and Alicia dropped a dainty curtsy towards her partner. Sir Hobart stood swaying slightly, but as the music began he moved almost as an automaton and with some help from the other dancers they began—right-hand star, left-hand star. The men linked arms and crossed to pass between the line of women with a little kicking step, then the women passed between the men. Sir Hobart took Alicia's hand in his and led her down the set and back, then with his hands on her waist and hers lightly resting on his shoulders there was a swing. His intoxicated breath was sour in her face, his hands seemed to drag down at her waist, his feet moved as if leaden, so that for her there was no pleasure in the dance.

Together they carried on, progressively down the ever-changing line of dancers, her partner's steps stumbling more and more heavily. Alicia's feet were bruised, her body aching from the effort of half-supporting the heavy weight of her partner's body as he swayed with less and less control.

Then he collapsed—Alicia could hold him no longer. She was aware that his legs were buckling beneath him and two of his servants appeared to take hold of him. Suddenly the weight of his heavy form seemed to be thrust aside.

Alicia was scarcely aware of what had happened for in that same instant her waist was grasped by hands that lifted her and whirled her around. She responded instantly, instinctively, her feet matching the deftly stepping ones that capered lightly to the rhythm of the dance, her hands were holding a pair of broad shoulders and she found herself gazing with amazement into a smiling face.

It was the stranger from the woods. Her mouth opened in a gasp; she almost cried out in her surprise, but he made a small pursing of his mouth and shook his head conspiratorially, warning her to keep quiet. How different it was to be dancing with him! Immediately she matched the lightness of his step as he swirled her on down the line of dance. She scarcely dared to glance into those smiling brown eyes, but when she did she read therein a joy that was a counterpart to her own.

Yet her heart was beating too fast for comfort and her mind was in a turmoil. Who was he, this stranger, who kept arriving to disturb her life? What was he doing here? Was he safe? He was no longer clad in peasant's garb, his tunic and his stockings were similar to those worn by the other young men of rank who made up her uncle's household and also those who had accompanied Sir Hobart. Over one shoulder hung a dashing short cape of dark red material.

The dance finished. Alicia looked around her anxiously, expecting her aunt to be there admonishing her for leaving her betrothed, but all attention was centred on Sir Hobart, who was seated on the bench by the fire again. Attending him was Uncle Rufus's physician. He offered a draught from a phial, only to have it dashed from his hand as the old knight shouted abuse.

'I don't want that muck. Give me some more malmsey.'

Thankful no one was watching her, Alicia looked up at the stranger who still held her hand. He drew her gently to one side until they were hidden from the main concourse in the hall.

'What are you doing here?' she asked breathlessly.

'Is it not obvious? I came to see you again.'

There was mockery in the smile he gave her, and then he raised her hand to his lips and kissed it; the

sensation was delightful, but it frightened her too—
she tried to pull her hand from his grasp but he
seemed loath to part with it, holding it firmly.

'You must not speak and act so foolishly,' she
whispered, glancing anxiously around.

No one was watching them. He pulled her
further into a darkened corner of the hall.

'Lady Alicia—I have heard that you are to be
married to that drunken sot—tell me it's not true?'

Without meeting his eyes she nodded her head.

'It is sacrilege,' he exclaimed. 'Think what your
life will be like!'

Then she looked up at him and, though his face
was lost in the darkness, the flicker of the candles
just beyond highlighted the handsome lines of his
head, so that she could almost see those manly
features that had haunted her all day. His presence
was as pleasing to her as ever—more so in his
finery, with that circular cape thrown nonchalantly
over one shoulder. He knew how to carry himself
well and proudly. Everything about him contrasted
so strongly with Sir Hobart that her despair
deepened. She heaved a sigh.

'I can think of little else. Believe me, this union is
not of my choosing. I would that it were not so, but
I have to obey.'

'And of course you will obey—what a biddable
little wife you will make.' His voice had more than a
touch of sarcasm.

'How can I defy them?' Tears started into her
eyes. 'They will beat me and starve me until I
agree.'

He ran a finger down her cheek.

'I'd take you to wife myself if there was any
chance your uncle would be willing.'

How differently she would feel if he was to be her proffered husband. Colour sprang hotly into her cheeks at the thought, but again she looked around fearfully.

'Who are you?' she asked.

'Sir Richard Calder, of Leet Castle.'

Alicia drew in her breath sharply. She had heard that name on her uncle's lips, spoken with venom, as a personal enemy, and a Yorkist as well.

'I see you have heard of me.'

'You should not be here. It is dangerous,' she whispered urgently.

He seemed in no hurry to leave.

'I have a great desire to carry you away with me. I wonder—would you come willingly?'

'Pray do not talk such nonsense. You know I am promised in marriage to Sir Hobart.'

'But there is no joy in that for you.'

'My uncle talks of you as an enemy. He would never give his consent—'

'I would have you, with or without his consent. Come—let us elope—'

'Sir! You presume too much!' Alicia drew herself up haughtily. 'You should not have come here. How did you manage to get into the castle?'

He gave a light chuckle.

'It was not too difficult. The knights who came with Sir Hobart are not all known to your uncle—with the one set I pass myself off as a neighbour of Rufus and with the other pretend that I have accompanied that old reprobate.'

'You are foolish to take such risks.'

'Needs must. There were—things I had to find out. And then—I wanted to see you again. I have been unable to concentrate my mind on anything but you since our meeting in the woods this morning.'

She hung her head. So it had been with her, but modesty prevented her from saying so. He needed no words to assure him, however; he took her pleasure in him for granted, assumed that the affinity between them was as natural to her as to him.

'Do not agree to this marriage,' he whispered urgently. 'Come away with me.'

'We would never get out of the castle—'

'There are ways—trust me—'

Her heart would gladly have acceded to his request but commonsense told her it was impossible. They would have no chance of reaching even the outer courtyard before they were stopped. The drawbridge was raised for the night; escape would be impossible.

'My lady—' Jenny's voice interrupted in a whisper.

The maid appeared so suddenly and silently that Alicia was startled. Jenny must have known where she was, must have been standing guard like the kindly angel she was—but now she hissed urgently.

'My lady—you must hasten back to Sir Hobart.' Then, to Richard, 'Sire—you have been recognised. They are preparing to search the castle for you.'

Richard stiffened immediately. Alicia felt the alertness of his stance and terror gripped her.

'Go—at once,' she implored.

'Remember what I have said. Come to me if you can. Adieu, sweet Alicia.'

He disappeared into the shadows, moving with such speed and stealth that she was scarcely aware in which direction he had gone. Only a sense of increased anxiety, of being bereft, told her that he had left her.

'My lady—come back into the centre of the hall. They are asking for you, too.'

Jenny pulled at Alicia's arm and together they stepped back into the room.

'If they ask questions we will say we have been attending to my toilette—that I had trouble with my headdress,' Alicia said.

'Yes, my lady.'

Jenny followed a pace behind, as Alicia made her way forward to where the glow of the candles seemed almost as bright as day after the shadowy corner where she had tarried with Richard. The great hall was surging with movement and angry shouting voices.

The men had armed themselves with swords and bows and arrows, with staves and pikes, and with a noisy stamping of feet and clanking of metal were rushing towards the exits. No one had time to bother about Alicia—she was almost pushed aside in the rush. It was Richard they were after and, with drink and a blood-lust coursing through their veins, they were eager for the manhunt.

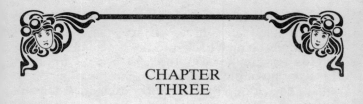

CHAPTER
THREE

THE SEARCH seemed to go on and on. Alicia had moved over to a bench and forced herself to sit beside the other ladies, listening to their conversation as if the matter was of no great interest to her, though her hands plucked restlessly at her skirt.

'The audacity of the man!'

'Such foolhardiness. I shouldn't like to be in his shoes when they capture him.'

'Just fancy! A spy in the castle.'

'And you danced with him, Alicia! Did you not know who he was?'

'How could I? I imagined everyone who was here was by my uncle's invitation,' Alicia replied.

If she sounded a little breathless, that was merely taken for astonishment at learning the identity of her partner.

'You should have left the dance when Sir Hobart was—er—taken ill,' grumbled Aunt Margaret.

'But I had no idea he was unwell. I simply imagined that he had tired of dancing and—and wished one of his young squires to partner me so as not to spoil the line of dance,' Alicia replied.

'You're a fool,' Aunt Margaret snapped.

What more she might have said was lost as a group of men returned to the great hall. Alicia scanned them anxiously, dreading to see Richard being dragged along with them, taken prisoner or even—dead. He was not with them and her heart steadied itself once more. There was anger and outrage on the men's faces.

'He's escaped. Got away—it seems he left through one of the back doors.'

'But the drawbridge was up,' exclaimed Uncle Rufus.

'One of the servants said he heard a splash—he must have dived in and swum the moat.'

'Someone must have warned him.'

Angry faces glared around.

'Who? Tell me who and I'll have him whipped within an inch of his life.'

Alicia shivered. That was no idle threat. But still her heart sang. Richard had got away—he was free. If only she could have gone with him—but she stilled such a foolish thought before it even had a chance to take root in her mind. She could never have escaped in that way. Had she tried to go with him she would only have added to his danger; besides, it was such an improper suggestion! It was unthinkable for a young lady in her position.

'Ale—let's have more ale to warm us.'

The mugs were soon replenished; the rushing about in the cool of the night had partially sobered the men, but it took only a few quaffs from their frothing tankards to re-ignite the fires of the brew, and the voices rose high and higher as the exploits of the night became more and more exaggerated in the telling.

At first Alicia scarcely listened, she was so relieved that Richard had escaped, but soon she began to catch the gist of the talk that was being bandied around her.

'He'll pay for this.'

'Spying—that's not the act of a gentleman.'

'But then, he's no gentleman, is he? A bastard, that's what he is—born the wrong side of the blanket.'

'He has no right to those estates—it's time he was put properly in his place.'

'With the men that Sir Hobart has brought—and there is another troop on the way—we'll outnumber him ten to one, and we'll give no quarter when we move in to take Leet Castle. It's time that young upstart was taught a lesson or two.'

'Bastard he may be—we'll make him wish he had never been born.'

As she listened wide-eyed, Alicia's fears returned. It seemed that Richard had escaped from the castle only to face more trouble. Her fears for his safety gave her courage to ask Aunt Margaret more about him.

'Who is he, Aunt Margaret?' she asked.

'Richard Calder. He's little more than a robber—he's taken it upon himself to claim Leet Castle—'

'And Draston Manor and they do say more lands besides,' put in another lady.

'Leet should have gone to your uncle,' said Aunt Margaret. 'He was promised it by the Duke for the help he gave in the battle of St Albans in 1455, but it seems this young upstart has moved in and occupied it. He won't be there long,' she added grimly. 'Now that we have the aid of Sir Hobart it will be a simple matter to attack it and take it from him.'

'Whatever made Richard Calder think he had a right to the lands?' Alicia pretended a dismay she was far from feeling.

'You may well ask—just because he claims that the Duke of Ranworth was his father. I'd like to see his mother's marriage lines! And the man's nothing but a roistering blaggard himself,' she added, pursing her lips in a grim line.

'Is—is he married?' Alicia ventured to ask.

'Not yet—though they do say that he has been seeking a match with the daughter of Lord Pennington. They'll hardly welcome such a marriage when he finds himself landless.'

So the talk went on and Alicia found herself torn between a yearning to know more, doubts as to where the truth lay and a growing dismay as everything she heard seemed to be more and more distasteful, more terrible, awoke more and more fears in her heart. Only one thing was certain, the attack would not take place until the additional troops had arrived, so there were a few days' grace. If only she could get a message to Richard—warn him of the great danger he was in.

It was awful to be a woman and so helpless—there was nothing she could do, either to assist Richard or to resist her own dread fate. Through the next day the talk of the impending assault on Leet went on, and so did the plans for her marriage. The sight of Sir Hobart in broad daylight made that proposition even more distasteful, hateful even, than it had been when she had first seen him in the dim light of the great hall.

His face seemed uglier, his figure even more ungainly and his disposition, still barrel-fevered from last night's excesses, brutish and coarse. A frantic desperation choked and terrified Alicia's heart and mind.

'What ever am I to do, Jenny?' she moaned when

she was alone with her maid. 'How can I escape this marriage?'

Jenny could only shake her head in sympathy. At that moment she was glad that she herself was not of noble blood, there was nothing to be gained from her marriage and, since she was in love with one of the young grooms, she was able to look forward to a future with Reuben, working together in service.

'When you marry I'll come with you, my lady,' she said. 'And if you will arrange it so that Reuben may come also, we would both serve you with our lives, if need be.'

Dismally Alicia nodded. 'Of course you must stay with me, always. You are my personal maid, and that will be some comfort. But, oh—I am so fearful for the future. It's not fair that I should have to accept such a man. How can they be so cruel? If only it were someone more like Richard Calder—I could go then so happily.'

'My lady—you must not speak so. 'Tis no use even thinking such thoughts. Perhaps it will not be so bad as you think.'

'Sir Hobart is so ugly—I hate him. I can scarcely bear to look at him and the thought of him touching me—' She broke off with a shudder.

'Many a woman has just to shut her eyes, mistress. I think he will be kind to you—if you comply with all his wishes, there will be no reason for him to beat you.'

'If only I could believe that!' exclaimed Alicia. 'But you know I have never found it easy just to comply. I shall be bound to say or do something that will reveal to him how I really feel.'

Jenny sighed. She was only too well aware of her young mistress's rebellious streak. She too had suffered because of it more than once in the past, being blamed for escapades that Alicia rushed into—no notice was ever taken of her protestations that Jenny had had no part in them—yet she remained steadfastly close beside her. The relationship between them had developed much closer than that usual between mistress and maid-servant, because neither of them had living parents. In times of trouble each had come to turn to the other for support and neither had ever found the other wanting.

It was after a second evening spent in the great hall, when she was compelled to sit close beside Sir Hobart and endure his unwelcome embraces—though convention prevented him from doing more than keep an arm tight round her waist and occasionally steal a kiss on her cheek—that Alicia determined that she would sooner die than ally herself in marriage to him. It was that desperation that drove her to formulate a plan of escape. She confided it to a terrified Jenny as soon as she was able to leave the company of the gentlemen and slip away to the quiet of her bedroom.

'Jenny—tomorrow I shall run away,' she announced.

Jenny glanced anxiously around her as if she thought the very walls might have ears to hear such talk.

'But, mistress—how can you—?'

'I have a plan. The men are going hunting at daybreak, and I shall go with them.'

'You would never be allowed.'

'They will not know it is I. I shall be dressed as one of them—I shall attire myself in tunic and hose, aye, and a hat with a brave feather which will cover all my hair.'

'Oh, no, my lady—it is far too dangerous. Besides, where would you go?'

'I shall ride to Leet Castle—to Richard Calder. I care not for the conventions. I will not marry that horrible old braggart—he has been telling me all evening how he will sack the property of Sir Richard—and kill him—and have his—his head displayed on a pike above the gateway.'

'And like as not he will,' Jenny said grimly. 'Where will you stand then, my lady?'

Alicia's heart sank. That was a prospect she dared not think about, but it made her more determined than ever. She clasped Jenny's hands and drew her down to sit on the bed beside her.

'If I warn him, there is a chance he may be able to send for reinforcements. He can at least prepare to stand siege. Oh, Jenny—don't you see I must take this information to him, and I must leave here myself. I cannot bear to live as wife to that—that monster. I would sooner die; so, I pray you, help me to get some clothes that will disguise me well. Please Jenny—do this for me.'

'Mistress, if you are determined to go, then I must go with you.'

'You said yourself, it is dangerous.'

'I know. But I can't let you go alone—besides, think what I should suffer here when they discovered you had left!'

Alicia had been walking restlessly up and down the room, now she ran to clasp Jenny's hands in hers. 'Forgive me—I—I had forgotten—of course you must come with me—but would you dare?'

'I would dare anything rather than stay here without you, my lady.'

'Bless you, Jenny, but can you help me to arrange it?'

'Aye, but I'll have to take Reuben into our confidence, for we shall need his assistance to get horses saddled in the morning.'

'Can he be trusted?'

'He will do it for me,' Jenny said simply. 'We have already plighted our troth. He may be fearful, but he will know that I shall be in terrible trouble if our plan is revealed. Indeed, I imagine he will be one of the retainers who accompany the hunt, so he will have no difficulty in getting out of the castle.'

'Tell him I shall reward him,' Alicia said. 'He will never be able to return to the employ of my uncle, and should the adventure not go well you would need to make your way to some town and make a new life there. I have no money, but give him this ring—it is of gold and has some value. Tell him there will be more if he helps us and keeps silent.'

'There is no need, my lady—'

'Take it—it is little enough.'

With some reluctance Jenny took the ring that Alicia thrust into her hand.

'I insist. Go now. There is no time to lose if we are to make our plans properly and still get some rest this night. We shall have a long day ahead of us tomorrow.'

Alone in her chamber Alicia removed her fine garments and folded them away. It was strange to do so herself, but Jenny had more than enough to attend to that night, and there was no other way Alicia could help her. She climbed into the bed, shivering slightly with cold and excitement and apprehension.

Time seemed to hang endlessly as she huddled

beneath the blankets, the feather-bed beneath giving a welcoming warmth. It was perhaps an hour or more later that Jenny returned, carrying a bundle of clothes.

'My lady—all is arranged. I have the garments for us both, and Reuben will have horses saddled ready for us. He is to accompany your uncle's knights tomorrow, so he is in no danger—and if we are caught before we leave the castle I have sworn that I will say that I saddled the horses myself. I do know how to, for as a child I spent a great deal of time playing in the stables and sometimes the grooms allowed me to help them.'

'Good. But after we leave the castle—will Reuben join us then?'

'Yes, my lady. You are to pretend your horse has gone lame and drop behind. Then Reuben will turn round to assist you. What is more, he says he knows a short-cut to Leet Castle. With luck and hard riding we could be there before dark.'

Long before daybreak Alicia and Jenny were busy attiring themselves in the unfamiliar clothing. It seemed to Alicia that she had not slept a wink all night, but she did not feel in the least tired, excitement stirred her blood, her every sense seemed to have an added keenness as if a magic potion flowed through her veins. Jenny bustled about clicking her tongue anxiously over fastenings, nervousness making her fingers unusually clumsy, yet driving her to scrupulous care that the identities of both Alicia and herself were well hidden.

Thank goodness the fashion was for padded shoulders to the tunics of the young men—that at least gave her a false look of manliness, while her narrow waist was adequate for the wide leather

belt, and the sword hanging there added a swashbuckling effect. True, her shapely legs looked
rather too feminine in the tight hose, and the
full-skirted tunic barely covered her rounded hips,
but that could be hidden by a cloak and in the
half-light before dawn it was likely that little attention would be paid to them.

Jenny looked like a page-boy—rather younger
than usual, but there was no help for that. Alicia
stood by the window till she heard the sound of
horses being moved about, neighing, hooves clattering on the cobbles and the voices of men, a
shout, a burst of laughter.

'Now,' she said. 'It is time to go.'

She did not even glance around the bed-
chamber; it had held little happiness in the years
she had occupied it. But she took Jenny in her
arms and kissed her on both cheeks, hugging her
close.

'Bless you, Jenny—God be with us.'

'Amen to that, my lady.'

It proved to be surprisingly easy to reach the
castle courtyard. The darkened passages hid them
well and, when spoken to, Alicia answered only
with a grunt which caused one young man to laugh.

'Still suffering from last night's ale, I'll warrant,
eh?'

Reuben waited for them with horses saddled. He
had not dared to make ready the little grey mare
which Alicia usually rode, for fear that it might be
recognised by her uncle or one of his men. He
cupped his hands and helped her to swing up into
the saddle. She had often ridden astride, refusing to
use the side-saddle though that was considered
more ladylike.

'She's a quiet enough mare,' Reuben whispered. 'But she's got plenty of go in her.'

'Thank you, Reuben.' Alicia kept her voice low, though she was a little distance from the other riders.

As soon as Jenny was mounted she moved nearer to where the young men were gathering their horses, hooves clattering impatiently as the animals were held reined in. One reared and caused some consternation.

'Get that drawbridge down and let's be off,' called one knight.

They were eager for the chase, men and horses alike, with the dogs keeping just clear of the horses' legs and servants handing up stirrup cups to fire the men still further. Alicia waited as impatiently as any and at last her uncle gave the order and the clanking of the machinery heralded the raising of the portcullis and the lowering of the great drawbridge and they moved noisily away into the soft morning air. The sun was just beginning to streak the east with gold.

At first Alicia and Jenny rode close to the band of horsemen, but gradually as the foremost broke into a gallop and the others took up the extra speed, the two girls allowed themselves to be overtaken by the excited young men until they were cantering along well back in the field. Alicia glanced back to make sure they were out of sight of the castle, hidden, even from any lookouts on the tower, by a group of trees and then she reined in. Jenny also halted.

'Now is the time, I think,' said Alicia.

Jenny dismounted and lifted one of the horse's legs, as if looking for an injury. Just as they had planned, Reuben galloped back to their assistance.

One of the huntsmen looked back but fortunately decided it was none of his business to go to the assistance of Alicia. They all carried on, riding fast away, careless that already one of their number had met with some mishap. Soon the hunt had raced out of sight.

'I understand you know a short-cut, Reuben,' said Alicia. 'You lead on.'

'This way, my lady.'

The morning was brilliant, the tracks were all rough, rutted but less muddy than they usually were, and it was possible to make good time. Jenny had thoughtfully brought with her a bag in which she had placed bread and cheese and a leather bottle of water. They shared this at midday and gave the horses a rest, allowing them to graze by the roadside and to drink from a nearby stream.

Then they were in the saddle again and riding as fast as the road conditions and their mounts could take them, mindful that they must try and reach Leet before nightfall. Robbers lurked in the woods and would be more likely to strike after dark, though one had to take care at all times. It was a comfort to have Reuben with them—what was more he seemed to know the way quite surely. When it got to late afternoon, however, and the castle was still not in sight, Alicia began to feel anxious.

'How far have we to go, Reuben?' she asked.

'I am not exactly sure, my lady, but I believe it cannot be far now.'

They spurred their horses on until they reached the top of a rise and there they reined in.

'There it is, my lady—over there.'

The sun was low in the west and cast golden red

light over the sleeping landscape. Some peasants were at work in the open fields and oxen grazed by a winding stream. Half a dozen clay-lump thatched hovels were clustered around the outer walls of the tall-towered castle and its windows twinkled as they caught the rays of the setting sun. It was a scene of beauty and tranquility.

'That's Leet,' said Reuben, triumphantly.

Alicia sat still, staring. Now she was here, she was strangely uneasy. What would Richard think of this escapade of hers? Suppose he had not really meant it when he had asked her to run away with him? What did she know about him? Doubts came crowding in on her.

'Come, my lady—we must hurry,' cried Jenny. 'It will soon be dark.'

Alicia touched her horse with her heels and, as if she knew there would be rest and food down there, she trotted off obediently in the direction of Leet. A great weariness began to take hold of Alicia. Though she was quite accustomed to riding from manor to manor three or four times a year when the whole household moved, or when they visited the households of other great lords in Norfolk, such travels were always undertaken in a much more leisurely way. Never before had she ridden so far and most certainly never at such a great speed. Allied to that was the effect of having had virtually no sleep the previous night and the constant fear of danger of discovery which had scarcely ever left her since she had donned those masculine clothes at such an early hour that morning.

All these things now closed upon her, making her slump in the saddle, so that it was only with a very sustained and concentrated effort that she man-

aged to remain sitting upright. At walking pace
they approached the main entrance of the castle,
where they were confronted by the joists of the
underside of the drawbridge uplifted and unwelcoming.

'Ho, there,' shouted Reuben to the armoured
men who gazed suspiciously down at them from the
guardhouse by the towers into which the huge chain
mechanism disappeared. 'We are friends, bringing
messages from afar for my lord Calder.'

'Whence come ye? State your name and business.'

Reuben turned to Alicia. She lifted her head
proudly.

'Tell them who I am.'

'This is Lady Alicia Bartolf and we are her
servants. My lady desires urgent consultation with
your lord.'

'I see no lady.'

Alicia could stand no more of this prevarication.
She would fall from the saddle if she were not able
to dismount soon. She lifted her hand and swept the
cap from her head, dislodging the pins in her hair to
allow the golden tresses to cascade down the shoulder of her tunic.

'Open up at once, or you shall answer to your
master for this delay,' she cried.

There was a gasp from one of the guards—a stir
of excitement.

'Faith, it be a woman, dressed as a boy. I reckon
there can be little harm in letting them in.'

'It may be a trick. Best to call the Captain
first.'

Alicia chafed impatiently as there was another
delay, but within minutes a tall, grey-haired man

appeared among the guards. He peered anxiously, doubtfully, into the twilight.

'Open at once,' demanded Alicia. 'My lord, your master will be angered that we have been kept waiting.'

The Captain nodded briefly to the guards and with a mighty rumbling and clanking the great drawbridge was lowered. The guards stood solidly flanking the entrance and kept a strict watch to make sure there was no trickery, no other army of followers waiting to charge the castle, and Alicia and her servants rode into the courtyard. A groom ran up to catch the reins of her horse. The Captain of the Guard himself came forward and held up his arms to help her to dismount and gratefully Alicia dropped into them.

'So, you are the Lady Alicia Bartolf,' he said. 'Whence come you?'

The Captain, who bore himself with a distinguished air, was a man of middle years, stern of visage.

'I have ridden here straight from Braister. I have important news I must tell your master. Take me to him at once,' Alicia commanded. 'And bid your men to see to my servants and to my horses.'

The Captain issued a few curt orders so that she was assured that they would all be well taken care of, then, with a charming gallantry, he offered his arm and personally escorted Alicia into the castle. Darkness had by now completely shrouded the countryside; within the stone-walled passages candles had been lit in the wall sconces. He led her straight to the huge main room and Alicia felt a fluttering of excitement at the prospect of seeing Richard Calder once again.

What would be his reaction? She wished she were not so travel-stained—what sort of a figure must she present in her boy's hose and tunic? But she must brave it out and trust that those words he had uttered, inviting her to run away with him, were truly meant. In any event she had a message of great import—she must tell him without delay of the proposed attack upon his stronghold here and of the additional men that would be joining her uncle's and Sir Hobart's force in only a few days from now. That thought lent a final surge of strength that allowed her to remove her hand from its resting-place on the Captain's supporting arm, to lift her head proudly and to step forward as if she were indeed a boy messenger.

Into the great hall she walked, and all eyes of the assembled company were turned towards her. She saw only that Richard Calder sat in a stiff-backed armchair close to the blazing log fire. She saw him start to his feet at her entrance.

'Well, Brian,' he said. 'Whom have we here?'

'A young lady who craves audience with you, Richard,' replied the Captain.

From the familiarity of their manner of address to each other it was evident that there was some bond between the two men beyond that of master and servant. Alicia continued to walk towards Richard.

'My lord,' she said. 'I bring news of the armies of my uncle, Rufus Blount, and Sir Hobart Kimball.'

'What news is this?' he asked.

His voice sounded puzzled; he signalled a servant to move a lit candelabrum closer so that he could see the face of this messenger, this boy with the long golden hair, whose voice sounded strangely familiar—and so feminine.

'Lady Alicia!' he exclaimed.

Just as the light glowed on her face, so it also illuminated that of Richard. He stared at her in astonishment, with distrust—and with no sign of welcome. He glanced behind her, as if he expected her to be followed by a host of enemies.

'Why have you come?' he asked.

His tone was cold, it was as if she was face to face with a different man from the one she had met in the woods—he bore no resemblance to the gay cavalier who had swept her off her feet in the dance. The only emotion on his face now was wary suspicion. Tears started into her eyes, her pent-up emotions, her fatigue from the journey, her disappointment at this reception welled up as if they would engulf her. She struggled to answer his question but no words would form on her lips. Her legs began to buckle beneath her. The Captain of the Guard reached out to steady her and she was grateful for the strength of his arms.

'Sit her down,' Richard commanded.

She was helped to a bench, but even as she sank down gratefully she noticed that another chair, set close beside that of Richard, held the figure of a woman. The elegance of the lady's dress of deep red threaded with an elaborate pattern of gold spoke of her wealth and rank, but, more than that, she was young and undeniably beautiful and she was seated close beside the chair in which Richard himself had been reclining. What scene of domestic bliss had she interrupted with her precipitate entry?

'Your news? Tell me your news?' Richard urged.

Alicia turned dark-ringed eyes towards him.

'They are planning an attack—in a few days' time—'

'This I know,' he said impatiently. 'It was to seek information of this that I obtained entry into Braister—but what other news have you?'

'There are reinforcements on the way. Another five hundred men belonging to Sir Hobart.'

Richard stamped restlessly across the room and back.

'Five hundred, you say?'

Alicia nodded, too miserable to speak.

'And when will they reach here?'

'That I—I know not, my lord.'

Impatiently he turned from her, making her feel that the information she had brought was worthless to him. He strode away again and spoke with his Captain of the Guard.

'You have heard what the lady says, Brian. It confirms what we already knew.'

'But it is possible the attack may come earlier than we expected,' replied the Captain. 'I know not how long we shall be able to hold out against such numbers, Richard, but we shall give a good account of ourselves.'

The Captain swung round and walked briskly from the hall; Richard moved back, not to Alicia, but to the lady who sat motionless, quietly observing the scene. He leaned forward and spoke to her confidentially, in a voice so low that none but she could hear, as if it was all-important to him that she should not be distressed by what had happened.

Then he returned again to Alicia and, as he came towards her, she was suddenly uncomfortably aware that, having revealed herself as a girl, it ill became her to be seated with her legs indecorously covered only by the hose. The skirts of her tunic were so short, in keeping with the current fashion of young men, that they barely covered the lower part of her body. Quickly she pulled the cloak closer round her to cover her knees—would that it would cover her face, too, for she felt ashamed of her dress and of her very presence here in Leet Castle.

What utter foolishness had brought her here! Richard had merely been playing with her, indulging in insincere flirtation, obviously that was all it was. His fireside was already graced by the beautiful lady who reclined there, serenely, regarding Alicia with an expression of amused surprise that in no way raised her confidence.

Who was that lady who occupied the position of honour in this household? The question battered like a hammer at her brain and in her state of weariness it seemed to make her head dizzy. The blaze of the fire, the flickering of the candlelight on the rich tapestries of the walls, the dark wood of the benches, the smell of roasting meat, all seemed to swim before her eyes, merging into an unsteady sea. She felt herself sliding from the bench on which she had been placed, her mind was slipping out of control. She felt faint and would have fallen to the floor had not a pair of strong arms caught her . . .

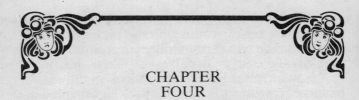

CHAPTER
FOUR

THE LONG hours of hard riding to which she was quite unaccustomed had taken their toll of Alicia. Exhausted, she had only a vague recollection of being carried up to a bed-chamber, of being laid gently on a soft bed—then had come complete oblivion. When she awoke, it was daylight. She moved a trifle stiffly and became aware that she was stark naked beneath the sheets. Suddenly wide awake, she opened her eyes and with the bed-covers pulled high beneath her chin, looked apprehensively around.

She was lying on a large four-poster bed, the heavy curtains closed completely making it into a rich tapestry box. Holding the sheet close to cover her bare breasts, Alicia pulled the curtains a little to one side and peeped out into the room. She could see no one. Where was Jenny, she wondered? Her maid always slept in the same room, at the foot of her bed.

'Jenny,' she called, softly at first and then again, rather louder. 'Jenny?'

There was no reply. Her mind darted back to the previous evening when she had fainted from sheer exhaustion; she remembered the comfort of those strong arms that had held her—Sir Richard had carried her up here, she was sure of that. Dimly as though through a veil she remembered distant voices and fingers that had fumbled with the fastenings of her garments—but who had undressed her? Somehow she was certain it had not been Jenny—then who?

A frown knitted her brow. Surely it couldn't have been—? The very thought that Richard had been there brought a flush of embarrassment to her face—but there was no way she could answer the question. Her arrival at Leet Castle had not turned out at all the way she had imagined it. What an utter idiot she had been to imagine that he would welcome her. Those words he had spoken had been but soft dalliance, meaningless pleasantries, that was quite obvious.

One person she certainly had not expected was that other woman, who had sat so comfortably at home there by Sir Richard's fireside. She was a woman of substance as well as of beauty—Alicia remembered those remarks of her aunt and the other ladies that Richard Calder had been seeking a marriage with the daughter of Lord Pennington. Perhaps those negotiations had been more advanced than Aunt Margaret had thought. News sometimes took a long time to travel, though at other times it was amazing how quickly word of mouth could transmit messages.

Whoever the lady was, one thing was certain, she had been a very welcome guest in Sir Richard's household and he had treated her with deference. Doubtless it had been her presence that had changed his attitude towards Alicia. Suddenly Alicia became devastatingly aware of how little she really knew about this tall, handsome autocrat who was her host. She had risked all in coming here, had put herself completely into his power—and that realisation made her extremely uneasy. What would happen to her now?

Since obviously there was no one else in the bed-chamber with her, Alicia stepped out of bed, wrapped a coverlet round herself and moved towards the window. The rushes strewn on the floor felt warm and soft to her feet. The sound of a door opening made her swing round sharply, clasping the cover still more tightly, intensely conscious of being naked beneath it.

'My lady.'

It was her maid who came in. She was carrying a tray with food and drink which reminded Alicia that she was very hungry.

'Oh, Jenny—how good it is to see you.'

'Are you quite recovered, my lady? They wouldn't let me in to see you last night; they said you were tired out and must sleep undisturbed. I was quite worried—you were all right, my lady?'

'I'm afraid I fainted and I'm not sure of anything that happened until I woke up a little time ago.'

Jenny smiled. 'You'll feel as good as new when you've broken your fast, my lady. Get back into bed and I'll set this tray on your knees.'

Alicia had no option but to obey; she realised that it was many hours since she had had anything to eat.

Jenny was wearing a dress of plain homespun, very similar to that she normally wore, though obviously it was not her own. She had nipped it in at the waist by tying an apron tightly around it and she had managed to find a piece of fine linen to fashion into a wimple for her hair.

'Can you find me something to wear, please, Jenny? My tunic and things are here, but I would prefer to revert to my normal feminine self. I have no wish to be for ever dressed as a man.'

'That you certainly cannot,' agreed Jenny. 'But I've already attended to that. I spoke to the other lady's maid this morning and she has left a complete set of garments for you. I'll fetch them while you eat.'

Jenny bustled off, seeming as blithe as ever and tending to Alicia just as if they had still been in Braister Castle. Her whole world was made up of Alicia and Reuben; so long as those two much loved people were close to her Jenny was content. When she returned she had clothes draped over her arms.

'Here, my lady.' She looked well pleased with herself. 'They are all perfectly clean—I looked to that and I think they will be quite becoming to you.'

The garments were of fine quality and Alicia would have been quite delighted with them, they were even more fashionable than those she was accustomed to—but they had belonged to that other woman. Richard might even have seen *her* wearing them—would that cause him to make a comparison? And if he did, how would she fare? That other woman began to assume an importance in Alicia's mind that was quite disproportionate to the amount she knew about her—which was virtually nothing. That lack of knowledge was in itself irritating.

'Jenny—who is she?'

'Do you mean the lady who left the castle early this morning?'

'There is no other, surely? The one whose clothes I am wearing—she seemed to be a person of consequence, tall, elegant—'

'That is so,' Jenny nodded. 'The lady set out with a large entourage at first light this morning.'

'She has already left?'

'Yes, my lady.'

'But who is she?'

'There was no mention of her name, my lady.'

'Do you know where she was going?'

'No one made mention of their destination, but they seemed prepared for a long journey. There was talk of getting the lady away to safety before the attack. Sir Richard sent some of his own men with her—'

'Surely he would not be so foolhardy! I'm sure he can ill afford to let any of his men leave here at this time. Does he not realise the strength of the attack that is imminent?'

'Oh, my lady—I don't know, I'm sure. God save us all.' Jenny looked wide-eyed and apprehensive. 'I only know Sir Richard was very worried about the lady. He kept saying again and again that they were to proceed with the utmost caution.'

For Jenny's sake Alicia calmed her fears, but that information was extremely disturbing—not least because the lady obviously meant a great deal to Sir Richard and that made her own future quite uncertain. Her impulsive act of running away had seemed to give her some control over her own destiny, more than she had ever had before—more than most females of her station in life could ever expect to achieve. She had fled from that hated marriage to Sir Hobart—but to what? By relinquishing the patronage of her uncle, she had put herself into a very compromising position. If Richard Calder was already married, if that lady

was his wife—or indeed if he had some other
amorous liaison—then what would Alicia's position in his household be?

That she was completely in his power she had no
doubt. She trembled a little at the thought. But at
the same time that wild streak which had impelled
her to escape to the woods outside Braister Castle,
leading to that first fateful meeting with Sir
Richard, came back to her strongly. She determined to seek him out immediately and to try to
ascertain more about this mysterious lady.

'Come, Jenny—we shall go and explore the
castle.'

Outside the quiet of the chamber in which Alicia
had slept so peacefully, all was bustle and movement. In the great hall the comings and goings
looked chaotic, but were probably quite ordered.
Wherever they went, preparations were being
made to withstand the coming attack. Provisions of
all sorts were being brought within the walls of
either the outer or inner courtyard. Animals were
being driven in from the surrounding farms, and
cartloads of corn and wood followed one after the
other. It was all being overseen by the castle
bailiff—there was no sign of Richard.

'Let us go up to the battlements,' said Alicia.

'Oh, my lady—do you think we should?' de-
murred Jenny.

'If you don't wish to accompany me, I shall go
alone.'

She sounded a little abrupt, but simply meant
what she said. She would not have been offended if
Jenny had not wished to accompany her, but her
maid's timidity would certainly not have prevented
Alicia from going.

'That you cannot,' said Jenny, with stout resignation.

Lifting her skirts just high enough to allow free movement of her feet, Alicia led the way up the winding stone stairs that led to the battlements. One room in the tower was used as an armoury and through the open door Alicia saw some men being kitted out with body armour. Stacks of pole-axes, lead mallets and pikes stood by the walls, together with long-bows, cross-bows and vast quantities of arrows. She could not help a shudder at the realisation that soon the fighting would begin and those weapons would be used to kill.

'It fair frightens me, let's go back,' entreated Jenny.

'I'm not giving up now,' said Alicia.

On she climbed up the uneven stone stairs, on and up and round until at last they emerged on to the roof of the highest tower in the western corner of the castle. The battlements were being prepared to repel the coming attack. Despite her fears to the contrary it was evident her warning had been taken seriously.

The roof of the tower was only a small circular area but it bristled with armaments. Sir Richard was organising the strategic positioning of a cannon which was being hauled towards a gun-port by a couple of men. The Captain of the Guard was also there and one man posted as lookout. A pile of huge round stones were ready to be loaded into the cannon and a barrel of gunpowder stood ominously ready. Neatly stacked by one wall were the soldiers' long-bows and a good supply of arrows, together with cauldrons of pitch and a brazier awaiting ignition.

Alicia watched for some minutes unseen by Sir Richard, who was dressed in a leather jerkin, his broad shoulders seeming more powerful than ever, a tall, commanding, handsome figure of a man. He was bare-headed, his dark hair tousled, his voice ringing out with an authority that demanded and received instant obedience. His whole stance was one of confidence, he knew what he was talking about when it came to a question of warfare, and his men respected him for it. That was evident.

Jenny pulled anxiously at her gown. 'Let's go back down, my lady. This is no place for us.'

'On the contrary, Jenny, I find it all most interesting. I wish to see more.'

As she spoke, Alicia stepped forward towards the battlements and stood looking out across the wide meadows that were so empty—and she trembled a little as she imagined the army of men that would soon be advancing to the attack against the castle. Although she had her back to him, Alicia was well aware that now Sir Richard was sure to see her.

'Lady Elizabeth.'

The word came from his lips, startled, horrified. It had been the dress he had recognised. Alicia swung round and faced him. His eyes were burning with excitement. The preparations for the coming battle seemed to have aroused every male instinct in him, there was an obsession with conquest; and in the way he looked at her she could feel how easily this intensity of awareness, of dedication to the demands of war could arouse in him an extra desire for the adventure of love and lust. He was so strongly masculine, standing tall and grim-faced, legs planted firmly apart, holding him rock-solid, towering over her. All that was feminine in her trembled beneath the coolly penetrating look that bore down on her.

She could return that steady gaze for only a few seconds, then perforce lowered her eyelids, bent her neck—training and etiquette came to her aid and she dropped the customary curtsy.

'Good-morrow, my lord.'

'You!'

The epithet was dismissive. No doubt it was disappointment that so hardened his voice.

'This is no place for women. Get below at once and say some prayers—for yourself if for no one else.'

She had no mind to be dismissed so lightly—that spirit that had given her strength to escape from her uncle refused to be quelled by Sir Richard. She lifted her chin in defiance but deliberately kept her voice even and calm.

'But, my lord, it is so interesting here. I am enjoying it immensely and the view is quite delightful.'

'It will be less delightful when we see the troops of Sir Hobart and Rufus Blount advancing towards us.'

'But that cannot be yet awhile. They were all at the hunt yesterday when I rode over to give you warning. And with most of the men on foot, it must be a few days before they will be ready to attack.'

'That is true, but we must not underestimate them. They are coming in force and I have few men at my disposal. I have to make very careful preparations or we shall be overwhelmed.'

'My lord—should you not send for reinforcements?'

'That I have done, but these are troubled times

we live in. I doubt my friends can muster many to my aid—besides I fear there is none close enough to reach us in time. Our success rests simply on our being well prepared.'

'Since that is so, I am amazed that you sent some of your men away this morning,' Alicia challenged, boldly.

'Who told you that?'

His voice blazed with quick anger. He was not accustomed to having his decisions questioned, that was obvious.

'No matter. Do you deny that when your lady guest departed at daybreak, you provided her with an additional escort?'

'I have no need to explain that to you or to anyone else. The safety of that lady is of paramount importance.'

'That is obvious,' Alicia responded with a toss of her head.

Richard regarded her keenly, and slowly his stern expression lightened as if some revelation had manifested itself to him. Then a corner of his lip lifted slightly and when he spoke he lowered his voice to a husky intimacy.

'Do I detect a note of jealousy, my lady?'

'Certainly not,' she flared at him. How dared he make such a suggestion! With a toss of her head she added—'Your affairs are of no concern to me.'

He continued to regard her with an expression of amused speculation. Embarrassment made red patches burn in her cheeks and her own temper flared up, the more so because it was possible that there was some truth in his surmise, unpalatable though it was.

'Ah—but you are wondering?' he murmured.

Alicia seized on the pretext of curiosity to recover her equilibrium and interrupted him with nervous eagerness.

'I—I merely thought that I had seen her somewhere before?'

'I think not.'

'One meets so many people—pray, what is the lady's name?'

'That I cannot divulge. It might affect her safety, and the fewer people who know her identity the less chance there is of her being involved. I beg you to ask no more.'

His mouth closed tight, making it impossible for Alicia to pursue the subject further. Sir Richard had decreed that the matter ended there and assumed that she would comply with that wish, but that certainly did not still her doubts and curiosity. Why he was so adamant that she did not, indeed should not, know the lady, she could not imagine. The one clear thing that had emerged was that the lady was not his wife—nevertheless he cared intensely about her, even to the extent of risking the safety of the castle to ensure her safety. Was he having an illicit affair with her? Was the lady perhaps married to someone else? Was Sir Richard simply an unscrupulous philanderer? What could be the reason for so much secrecy? Alicia did not know what to think. The one certainty was that the existence of that mysterious lady completely changed her relationship with Sir Richard.

'Does your uncle know where you are?'

Abruptly he threw the question at her, interrupting her reverie.

'I neither know nor care,' she replied, tossing her head.

'You arrived in disguise—tell me, pray, how did you escape from Braister?'

Alicia laughed at the recollection, pleased with herself for having duped them, and in graphic detail told him exactly how she had managed it. His face remained sober as he listened intently.

'No one at Braister knew of your destination? You confided in no friend, no servant?'

'No one at all, except for Jenny and Reuben who came with me.'

'And they are to be trusted?'

'Completely—with my life, if need be. Indeed I imagine my whereabouts must be causing my uncle some puzzlement.'

'It is important. If your uncle is aware that you have come here to me, then he will be all the more eager to sack the castle and recover his missing ward.'

'He cares not one jot for me.'

'Maybe not, but he has an interest in marrying you to Sir Hobart—'

'I would sooner die,' declared Alicia. 'Oh, sire— I dread to think what may happen should they recapture me.'

Momentarily she thought she read compassion on his face. His eyes raked over her; it was as though he were seeing her naked, stripped of the fine gown and the elaborate headdress that covered her so modestly. She blushed at his next words.

'Aye, in truth, you would make too lovely a bed-companion to be sacrificed to that old lecher.'

She knew then that Sir Richard would take her himself, if it were possible—and the recollection of her nakedness on awakening that morning increased her doubts of him. She was fairly certain it had been he who had carried her to the bed-chamber—had he stayed there while the women undressed her? There was no answer to that and he was now eager to return to those urgent preparations for the coming attack.

'My lady—we have tarried long enough. Go below, at once.'

'I have no wish to detain you. I shall stay here quietly and watch.'

'You shall not. You will go below.'

'No, sire. I did not escape from Braister to become a prisoner in another castle.'

Suddenly it was a clash of wills. Alicia had no intention of meekly obeying his command, she was not prepared to give way on this point—but neither was she prepared for his reaction to her obstinacy.

'Then I shall carry you.'

Suiting action to words he lifted her easily off her feet and, before she had recovered sufficiently from her astonishment, strode over the roof towards the stairs. Jenny, who was waiting there, regarded them wide-eyed. Alicia began to kick wildly.

'Put me down, you—you blackguard.'

'You did not struggle so when I took you up to your bed-chamber last night,' he grinned.

'Last night I was quite exhausted.'

'So—is that not good reason for you to rest today? I would not have you exhausted again this night. A man needs company and comfort on the eve of battle.'

'Sir—I am not to be trifled with,' she cried, kicking and struggling harder to prove the truth of her assertion.

His arms merely closed tighter round her, making her aware of her own frailty, crushed as she was so tightly to him, the slight muskiness of his tunic enhancing that aggressive animal maleness that it was impossible to ignore. Still she refused to plead with him and her voice snapped angrily.

'Let go of me this instant.'

He laughed lightly, as if he knew that he had her close to breaking-point, despite her command.

'I will, my lady—as soon as I have your word that you will return to the state apartments. Stay either in the solar or in your own chamber.'

To argue would have been foolish. Alicia was already conscious of the grins of the men who had turned from their posts at the battlements to watch this episode in the eternal struggle of male and female—this quite different warfare. There was no way she could win physically when this man was determined. His strength was the result of long, hard and continual training, his very survival must often have rested on his muscle-power, but to that strength was allied a formidable astuteness, an iron will and a quickness of reaction that were encountered but seldom and that made such a man outstanding among his peers.

'As you wish,' she said.

'It is for your own safety.'

He continued to hold her as if his arms were reluctant to release her, and his eyes seemed to bore deep into her inner being. Her heart was beating so fast she felt as if it would burst within her breast and the colour flared high in her cheeks.

When he had asked her to run away with him, she had supposed that it was an honourable arrangement—now that she was here, she was full of doubts. She still needed to know who was that lady who had been sharing his hearth with him last

evening? Worst of all was the fact that even if his
intentions were not honourable, her flesh was so
excited by the touch of his hands, by the pressure of
his chest—she could feel the hard bone of it pressing into the softness of her breast—that she might
find it impossible not to surrender to him. She felt
wanton—and was ashamed of herself. She pushed
her hands against his shoulders, trying desperately
to free her body from this so disturbing contact with
his.

'Set me down at once, sir.'

He gave a light laugh. It made her feel that he
understood all too clearly those racing emotions—
that it was only the conventional veneer of civilisa-
tion that made her demand her release. She was
horrified to find that there was a primitive core
within her that delighted in being handled thus. His
answer was to crush her closer in his arms, to hold
her so tightly that her body felt as if it must break—
and then abruptly he released her. That support
was taken away so suddenly that she tottered and
had to reach out a hand to the doorway to steady
herself.

Sir Richard took a step back, his eyes held hers
with a mocking smile as he swept his arm forward in
a wide gesture that carried all the grace of an
accomplished courtier and executed a deep bow.

'This evening, my lady, I trust we shall spend a
few pleasant hours together.'

She lifted her head proudly high, but no reply
would form on her lips. For once she was quite
speechless.

'Go! If I find you wandering about the castle
again, I shall have you locked in your chamber, and
I would not wish to do that.'

He turned on his heel and immediately, as if the incident with her had already been dismissed from his mind, resumed directing the dispersal of the armaments. Alicia had no choice but to do exactly as he had instructed her. He was Lord of Leet Castle and all who lived therein. His power was absolute. The very thought made her tremble. What manner of man was this into whose hands she had so recklessly placed herself? How foolish she had been to believe that he would marry her— because that was what had been at the back of her mind. She had nothing to offer him.

She had come to him penniless, without even a trousseau, clad only in the clothes of a young squire. No hope that her uncle would give her a dowry now—no doubt he had offered some worth- while inducement to Sir Hobart in recognition of the alliance that would be forged between their families, but he would certainly not be prepared to enter into any such arrangement with Sir Richard Calder. No man married unless it was for personal gain—or at least very few of them, and they were mostly scorned as fools by their peers. Marriages on the whole had nothing to do with love, but were almost entirely concerned with the accumulation of property and power.

It was in a very sober and serious mood that Alicia, followed closely by a much relieved Jenny, descended the cold stone steps and made her way along to the solar.

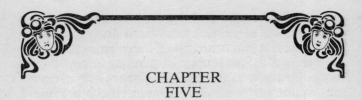

CHAPTER
FIVE

THE SOLAR at Leet Castle was on the first floor, reached by a wide staircase from the great hall, and it was one of the most beautiful rooms Alicia had ever seen. It was well proportioned, and its mellow roof built of huge dark timbers had been fashioned in the style known as collar-beam. Immediately opposite the door by which she entered was an oriel window, a rounded Gothic bay with delicate tracery. The sun glinted through its myriad diamond panes and lit with special brilliance the stained glass insets of armorial designs. The walls were plastered and hung with rich tapestries. Alicia wandered from one to the other of them, admiring how finely they were woven and guessed they had come from Arras in Flanders. There were two hanging on each side of the room, so large they almost covered the wall. They depicted scenes of country life, harvest, hunting, feasting and morris dancing.

There was a small collection of books. Alicia looked among them, selected one called *The Cronycles of France* and took it over to the comfortable chair by the oriel window. Jenny settled herself on a stool and produced a piece of cloth and thread and needle and began industriously to mend a torn shirt.

'That Reuben of mine, he's for ever rending his clothes. 'Tis all I can do to keep him decent,' grumbled Jenny as she set to work on the patch.

Alicia smiled. She knew that Jenny was really enjoying the performance of this small service for her beloved. She turned to the book and tried to concentrate but, though in normal circumstances she might have enjoyed reading it, today she found it impossible to keep her mind on it.

'Ouch! There—I keep pricking my finger—oh dear,' Jenny wailed. 'I don't know how you can sit there so calm, my lady.'

'What else can we do, Jenny? We must simply trust in God and in the defences of the castle. Sir Richard and his Captain of the Guard are making all possible preparations.'

'He's Brian de Warante, a distant cousin and absolutely devoted to Sir Richard,' Jenny remarked.

She had obviously been indulging in one of her favourite pastimes, chatting with her fellow servants, and already had unearthed several snippets of information that she was anxious to impart to her mistress. Alicia recognised the signs and was by no means loath to learn more.

'A cousin, you say?' she prompted.

'Well, it was the wife of Brian de Warante who was cousin to Sir Richard's mother. Her name was Beatrice, she was the daughter of a merchant, very comely, and the Duke of Ranworth fell in love with her.'

'With Beatrice?' Jenny's versions sometimes became difficult to follow. 'No, mistress,' Jenny replied with a touch of exasperation. It was all so clear in her head she couldn't see how she had confused the story. 'Beatrice was the wife of Brian de Warante. It was Sir Richard's mother that the

Duke of Ranworth fell in love with. I don't know what her name was. He wished to marry her, but he had been betrothed by his parents while he was still a child. It seemed there was no escape from that marriage for it was legally binding, though there was no love in it and the Duchess was a poor thing, half-crippled, they do say, so there could be no children from the union.'

'How very sad,' Alicia murmured.

'Yes, it was very sad but it seems that the bold young Duke won the heart of the merchant's daughter so completely that she ran away with him, but their happiness was brief. She died at the birth of her son—that was Sir Richard—and then the lady's cousin, Beatrice, who was wife to Brian de Warante, you remember, being barren herself took the babe and brought him up as her own.'

'Ah,' Alicia gave a sigh. 'I understand now why there is such familiarity between Sir Richard and his Captain of the Guard.'

'Many say that Sir Richard felt a greater love for Brian de Warante than he did for his own father,' nodded Jenny.

'That I can well understand. And what of Beatrice?'

'She died a few years back. De Warante was a most affectionate and faithful husband, they say, even though she never gave him a child of his own. Since then he's been entirely devoted to Sir Richard.'

Jenny had finished her story. She sat quiet for a few minutes and began again to work at the patch she was applying to Reuben's shirt. Alicia picked up her book and tried to read, but found it impossible to focus her mind on the words.

What would happen here in the next few days? Though she had heard many tales of skirmishes and sieges, she had never been closely involved in one. Would the attack succeed—or would the castle prove impregnable? Despite its meagre complement of men, it had been built on stoutly defensive lines, and Richard had seemed very confident and capable. Nothing in his speech or demeanour had suggested the possibility of defeat—pray God that all would go well with them. In any event, as she had pointed out, it was unlikely that the attack would come for a few days yet.

Again she tried to concentrate on her book but the words just swam senselessly before her eyes. The strong, rugged face of Sir Richard seemed to glare at her from the open pages, saying, *This evening, my lady, I trust we shall spend a few pleasant hours together*. She was not at all sure whether that was a prospect she should welcome or otherwise.

That Richard was free with his kisses had been manifested when they first met in the woods; that he was something of a lady's man she had realised when they had danced together. He had been accomplished in the art, not only of the dance itself, but also in the pleasantries, the dalliance, the light touches of hands, the sidelong glances, which were part of the social etiquette of flirtation. In every aspect he was a man that any woman should treat with respect and care. She was anxious that he should not think of her as a wench of little virtue who could be treated lightly. In case any such ideas were being harboured within that handsome head of his, Alicia decided to be on her guard, to keep her distance and respond to him in only the most formally polite terms.

Meal times at Leet Castle fell into the customary pattern to which Alicia was well accustomed. She had eaten in her room that morning so had not gone down for dinner at half-past nine. Soon now it would be time for the second meal of the day, supper, at five o'clock. An hour before then, Alicia repaired to her room and Jenny bustled away down to the kitchens to fetch hot water and, as soon as she returned, helped her lady with her toilette. Somehow Jenny even managed to procure a piece of fine linen, which she had starched with flour and water to stiffen into a fresh headdress for her mistress.

'How thoughtful of you, Jenny,' said Alicia, with appreciation.

Jenny smiled with pleasure. 'I thought that tonight it was especially important that you should look beautiful to please Sir Richard,' she said artlessly.

Her words brought a frown to Alicia's brow. 'I—I am not sure that I would not do better to make myself look ugly.'

'Oh, my lady—that would be impossible,' declared Jenny, loyally but also sincerely. 'You looked lovely even dressed as a boy—I'm quite sure Sir Richard thought so.'

'Jenny—don't talk like that.'

'But do you not wish my lord to fall in love with you, my lady?'

'No—I mean, yes—oh, I don't know. Oh, Jenny what an impossible position I have put myself in.'

'What do you mean, my lady? Did Sir Richard not invite you to run away with him when you talked together that evening in Braister?'

'Yes—but that was all he said. He made no

mention of marriage, and anyway I'm not at all sure now that he really meant it. I—I feel that since then he has given his heart elsewhere.'

'But my lady—there has been no time—'

'I had met him only briefly before he invited me to run away with him. I'm sure he has known that other lady for some time—it's obvious that he is deeply devoted to her. He told me that her safety was of paramount importance to him.' Alicia stamped her foot in a sudden surge of anger. 'Would that I had never warned him of the impending attack. Would that I had left them to face my uncle's forces together.'

Jenny looked horrified. 'Oh, my lady,' was all she seemed able to say.

'That is all that has come from my attempt to help,' Alicia fumed. 'He has simply used the time to send that—that woman to a place of safety, and even sent some of the few men he had here to guard her passage. What a fool I've been.'

'My lady, you must not speak so. I'm sure Sir Richard—'

'How can you be sure of anything about Sir Richard?' interrupted Alicia, her anger still boiling up in her. 'I wish I'd never come here.'

'But—but then you would have been married to Sir Hobart,' Jenny pointed out.

That was a sufficiently sobering thought to allow Alicia to calm down slightly. She said no more, but forced herself to sit quietly, allowing Jenny to make the finishing touches to her toilette while the towering headdress was adjusted so that the fine linen swung becomingly around her face. At last Jenny stepped back, nodding with approval and immediately Alicia leapt to her feet.

'Come,' she said. 'Let us go down.'

In the great hall preparations for the meal were well under way. The trestle tables had been erected and servants were setting out platters, bowls, knives and spoons. Sir Richard was sitting in that stiff-backed armchair before the fire, just as he had been on the previous evening. His legs were stretched out before him, he still wore the tunic of soft, supple, leather which seemed moulded to his strong body. No doubt the preparations for the coming siege were very much in his mind, but there was something reassuring about the sight of him looking so tranquil and thoughtful.

Hesitantly Alicia advanced towards him. She moved quietly in her flat-soled, soft leather sandals and had approached to within a few feet of him before he looked up. At first he seemed so far away, so deep in thought, that he had forgotten who she was. Momentarily he scarcely seemed to stir and she guessed that concern for the future lay heavy upon him.

Then, suddenly, his eyes danced to life, that old mocking expression leapt into them. He seemed to make a determined effort to throw care and responsibility away. With unhurried movements he stood up and stepped forward.

'My lady.'

Formally they exchanged a bow and curtsy and when Alicia looked up and met his eyes she saw in them an expression that went deeper than admiration for the gown and elaborate headdress that covered her so demurely from head to foot. His eyes strayed over her, taking in the delicate lines of her sweet face, the low-cut neckline of the *cotte* which revealed the firm flesh just above her round-

ed young breasts. Richard took his time in looking
her over, his reaction was one of sheer joy in an
object of great beauty—what troubled her was the
unmistakeable assurance in that look—it was a
possessive delight, as if she already belonged to
him.

He made no attempt to hide the slight smile of
sensual pleasure that manifested itself on his lips.
Sir Hobart had complained that there was not
enough meat on her—Sir Richard seemed to have
no such reservations—and Alicia, with a sense of
wonder that it should be so, knew that in each
of those very different men she could arouse a
passionate desire.

She had been sheltered by her upbringing in
many ways and this aspect of her burgeoning young
womanhood was one that had not manifested itself
until recently. She was not at all sure whether she
should welcome it as a blessing or fear its dangers;
most definitely it added complications to life.

Inevitably she had acquired a knowledge of the
facts of life, hearing and even sometimes seeing
bawdy encounters that went on in the kitchens and
in the fields between the servants—and indeed
often between the knights and the servants or even
the daughters of the tenant farmers. Little was
done to hide such carnal boisterousness—indeed it
was often thought to be no bad thing for the blood
of the knights to be seeded down to the villagers.

Yet always the emphasis had been that such
behaviour was quite alien to a young lady of good
family—and she had believed that it must be so.
Alicia's mind was in a turmoil as she encountered
that so very disturbing look in the eyes of Richard,
knowing how completely she was in his power,

dreading that he should take advantage of it and yet
unable entirely to suppress the excitement that he
roused in her.

She had read ballads of love, heard the minstrels
sing of it—had day-dreamed that one day it might
indeed come to her, but now, in recognising the
physical sensations that it roused within her, she
felt fearful. She wished that the tell-tale colour had
not flared so hotly into her cheeks, and she lowered
her gaze so that she seemed to be concentrating
entirely on the rushes strewn on the floor.

'Come, Lady Alicia—' Richard took her hand
and led her towards the chair where he had been
sitting. He indicated that she should seat herself on
a low stool close by.

'Have you any more news of—of the attack?' she
asked, making a valiant effort to keep her voice
steady.

'I am awaiting the return of scouts that were
despatched to reconnoitre some hours ago.'

She was glad that he answered her question
seriously and matter-of-factly, it enabled her to
assemble her emotions and her mind back to some
semblance of her usual serenity.

'Do you think you will be able to repel them?'

'That I cannot be sure. I have deployed my men
and armaments to the best of my ability, but I
cannot overlook the fact that I have far too few
archers and little or no explosive. We have, of
course, the advantage given us by the castle itself—
it has withstood sieges before now.'

'I shall pray for your success,' Alicia murmured.

'Aye, you do that. We shall need all the prayers
that can be said for us.'

'If only there was some way we could persuade my uncle not to attack.'

'Huh!' Richard's grunt made her conscious of her naivety. 'He knows full well that Leet is mine, left to me by the will of my late father, God rest his soul. But in these days of civil war, it is the strongest who take and for the weak there is no justice. When I heard of my legacy, I knew I had to occupy Leet myself immediately, for it was certain that Rufus Blount would dispute my right to it.'

'But if you are indeed the heir, surely you can prove that in the law courts?'

'I would have no difficulty in doing that, and if it should happen that their forces drive me from this place, then I shall ride at once to London and lay my claim there—always supposing I am not slain in the attack.'

Alicia blanched at the thought. Though she both feared and distrusted Sir Richard, the thought of his death was too shocking to contemplate. She swallowed the lump that suddenly rose in her throat. Richard shrugged.

'Life is sweet, I grant you,' he said. 'But I fear not death and if it comes whilst I am defending my rights, then surely that would be God's will.'

'Oh, my lord—you must take care. Would it not be better to leave the castle now—'

Alicia's fears made her speak without thought.

'Run away before I have even tasted the strength of their attack? That I will never do.' His eyes narrowed and he looked at her thoughtfully. 'If you are fearful, I could maybe arrange for you to leave on the morrow.'

'I have nowhere to go,' she replied with lowered

head, her voice barely audible. 'Except to a convent.'

'Nay. Such a bleak fate should not be for you, Alicia. 'Twould be sacrilege to rob mankind of such beauty.'

He must be laughing at her, of course, but she replied with quiet sincerity.

'I should prefer even that to marriage with Sir Hobart.'

'On the impossibility of your marriage to Sir Hobart, we are agreed, my lady. But let us have no more of this talk of defeat. I have no intention of handing my property over to those thieving swine.'

'Oh, my lord, they come in great strength and I cannot help feeling afraid. I have never been under attack before—'

'If the worst happens, don those male garments again and slip away to safety if you can. Though it still distresses me to think of those charms withering within the walls and dark habits of a nunnery. But let us not think on such dismal things. This night I shall keep you with me—a man needs a woman's company on the eve of battle.'

Alicia's heart thudded within her breast. What did he mean by those words? He would keep her with him—this night? She lifted her head and held it high. He caught the light of proud withdrawal in her eye and, to her amusement, he simply threw back his head and laughed.

'You are very young, Alicia. You know little of life. What a pleasure it will be to teach you. And—' he paused, leaned forward and with a tender touch ran one finger gently down her flushed cheek. 'And what pleasures there are of which to teach you.'

She was unable to look up at him and sat with

demurely lowered eyes, almost mesmerised, as if this man could exert a hypnotic influence over her. Then abruptly that note of near-tenderness left his voice and anger flared into its place.

'Have you nothing to say? Must you sit there looking like a sacrificial lamb? Your fears make you very poor company.'

'I—I'm sorry, my lord—'

'It's not sorrow, I need. It's some life and gaiety to dispel this blackness of mood.'

'Yes, my lord.'

What could she say to him? If only she were older and wiser—if only she understood him better. Abruptly he sprang to his feet and then she did look up and saw him glowering at her.

'It's time to eat. Come—let us to the table.'

Even as he spoke, he reached down that same hand that had just stroked her face and, grasping her hand, pulled her to her feet so firmly that she was almost catapulted into his arms. Keeping that hand held tightly in his, he led her towards the top of the long trestle table and seated her there on his left side. The place to his right was occupied by Brian de Warente. Even had Alicia not known of the bond between the two men, the affection and trust that each felt for the other would have been apparent in their manner and conversation.

There must have been close on seventy people eating there that evening. As well as Richard's guards, his soldiers and servants, the tenant farmers had been brought in with their families to help to defend their lord's property. Yet it was a pitifully small number in reality, for there were probably not more than two dozen fully able-bodied men among them, with another six posted on the towers to keep watch. Of the others, some men were quite old and frail and there were a handful of boys, not yet proficient in the use of the long-bow, and about thirty women and children, the usual female labour of dairymaids, laundresses and cooks.

Certainly the women had been busy in the kitchens and a succession of roast meats and savoury pies were carried in. Richard fell to eating at once and since he was so occupied Alicia found herself able to relax a little. The delicious smells made her realise she was more hungry than she had realised. She lifted the meat with dainty fingers and ate it with relish, accompanied by good home-baked bread and fresh butter, and sipped at frothing ale from a silver tankard.

Before the meal ended the minstrels in the gallery started to play. They were skilled in their art, making merry with rebec, harp, shawm and gittern, producing a rough and cheerful noise, though it barely cut through the sound of voices and the clatter of platters on the tables below.

Suddenly the double doors at the far end of the hall were swung open and in came two men dressed as foresters. Together they strode towards Sir Richard with the confidence of old and trusted servants. They were two of the scouts he had despatched to discover what they could of the enemy's movements. Each bent to one knee in customary obeisance to their lord.

'Rise. Tell me—what news?'

'They are on the march, sire—Sir Hobart Kimball and Rufus Blount with about twenty horsemen and nigh a hundred on foot. They are bearing arms. The first of them will be here by mid-morning tomorrow. The horsemen could be earlier, but it is likely that they will camp by the River Ripeley and move forward together. They bring provisions and arms, carts loaded with scaling ladders, gunpowder and battering rams.'

'You have done well—but where is Hugh Griffiths? Did he not go with you?'

'He did, sire—but we had a misfortune. We encountered some of Sir Hobart's men. They were an advance party sent out to make contact with more troops who are advancing from the west.'

'The devil take them,' Sir Richard swore.

'The two companies of men will meet up here and the attack will start as soon as they can assemble their forces.'

'Did you find out when?' asked Brian de Warante.

'Not to be certain, but it could even be tomorrow. They have recently been gathering reinforcements.'

'We shall have to use every subterfuge at our command. And Hugh?'

'Hugh fell into the hands of Sir Hobart's men. He was moving forward, several yards ahead of Edmund and myself, and it was as though they lay in ambush for him. He had no chance to escape, nor we to go to his assistance without being discovered ourselves, when we would surely have been overwhelmed. He was taken prisoner—and we were lucky to escape and we came here with all speed.'

'You did well. This information is essential. Now that we know the strength of our enemy, we can plan accordingly. Sit down, drink, eat and regain your strength.'

Sir Richard rose to his feet and addressed the assembled company. A silence had fallen whilst he talked to the scouts, though only those as close to them as was Alicia could have heard their messages. They did not need to hear the actual words to know that there would be no escape from the attack.

'There will be no dancing or merriment this night,' Sir Richard commanded. 'No more ale will flow, everyone to his bed betimes. You will need all your strength and fortitude to see you through the morrow. We do not expect an attack in darkness—but have no fears, sentries will be posted and if the trumpet sounds, then every man must be ready to repel the invaders.'

Sir Richard sat down again, pushed his platter aside and quaffed the last of the ale in his tankard.

Alicia trembled, her eyes were troubled and fearful as she gazed at him earnestly.

'My lord—you—you will take care?'

'Of that you may be certain. I had not expected the attack so soon—there will be no opportunity for you to leave before battle is joined.'

'It is as God wills. I am not afraid.'

'Well spoken. Should I fall tomorrow the castle would be possessed within the hour. Go to your room now and pray for us all.'

'That I will, Sir Richard.'

'Brian, let us check our defences once more.'

With that he stood up and followed by de Warente strode from the hall. He was the war-lord now, in command of his troops—that bright contentious light had flared into his eyes again. If the numbers had been more equal Alicia knew that she would have slept without the least qualm for her safety, without the slightest doubt that Richard could repel the attack and hold Leet Castle against the enemy. But those troops camped out in the countryside beside the river, as Edmund had reported, were barely five miles away. Tomorrow it would take them little time to cover that ground, they would still be fresh, they were said to be well equipped and, what was more, their numbers were many times greater, compared with the few men who were within the castle.

Alicia repaired to her room at once, Jenny following close behind her. After she had helped Alicia to undress and prepare for bed, the maid bobbed a curtsy.

'My lady—will it be in order for me to go below and talk with Reuben, just for an hour, perhaps?'

'Yes, of course, Jenny—but do not tarry too long.'

'Thank you, my lady.'

Jenny sped away and Alicia was left alone in her room, and at that moment she was almost envious of her maid's position, held close within the arms of her betrothed.

Then she pushed such unbecoming, immodest thoughts from her mind and knelt by her bed to pray, probably more fervently than she had ever done. She stayed there until the chill of the air penetrated her cotton shift, and shivering climbed into the big bed. It was impossible to sleep immediately. She lay awake listening until Jenny returned to curl herself on the rushes of the floor at the foot of the bed. Only then, with a sigh, did Alicia relax and drop off to a deep sleep.

In the morning there was activity all round the castle. Alicia was determined to see something of what was going on and again made her way up to the battlements—but this morning she had no intention of calling Richard's wrath down upon her-

self. She knew that he could not afford time even to
tell her to get out of the way, but her own wilful
curiosity could not be entirely repressed. As dis-
creetly as possible she climbed the steps to the great
tower and stepped out on to the roof.

Sure enough, there at the edge of the wood,
beyond the meadows which were kept clear of
anything that might make cover for an advancing
army, were the horses and accoutrements of Sir
Hobart Kimball. Alicia recognised his colours of
purple, green and white carried on a banner, recognised too his ugly figure slumped on a great char-
ger. Beside him was the taller figure that she knew
to be her uncle Rufus, the armour of both men
glinting in the sun.

They were beyond range of arrows or cannon-
fire from the castle. They were directing the movement of the men on foot, who were gathering into a
rough semblance of lines. Behind and below her
the castle was prepared for defence, the drawbridge to the outer court was raised and the portcullis down. Men were stationed all round the wall
walk with long-bows and cross-bows to be fired
from the arrow-slits and also with lead mallets,
pole-axes and bills, should the walls be breached or
scaled, to lead to close quarter fighting. A pile of
rounded stones stood beside each of the two can-
nons, together with barrels of gunpowder.

Richard stood, tall, straight, confidently gazing
to where the enemy were mustered, horsemen a
little to one side, foot soldiers waiting orders from
Sir Hobart, who was obviously in command. At the
sight of him, Alicia quailed.

Suddenly there came a shrill blast of a bugle,
there was a movement and the attackers ran for-

ward in a great company, their bows at the ready,
spread across the whole width of the field. Richard
gave the command and trumpets sounded from the
battlements, a tattoo rolled from a kettledrum to
warn the defenders to prepare for battle. As the
long-bowmen advanced they loosed a tremendous
flight of arrows which whizzed over the parapets of
the castle with such volume that the defenders had
to keep their heads behind the battlements.

Richard's men loosed back at them, using short
iron-headed quarrels in their cross-bows. Some of
the attackers fell, but the main body of men rushed
on; some bore shields and others carried planks
which served the same purpose but were also intended to build a rough raft for crossing the moat.
Richard directed the defence from the great tower,
while de Warante was on the western tower at the
corner of the outer court. Richard gave the order
for the cannon to be fired, the gunner touched it
with a lighted flare and Alicia covered her ears with
her hands against the explosion that made the gun
rock on its heavy wooden cradle. Smoke covered
the top of the turret. When it cleared, she could see
that the stone ball had cut a swathe through the
advancing men, and she was horrified to think of
the death, pain and suffering, even though they
were the enemy. Richard's eyes blazed with the
light of battle. He darted from post to post, gave a
brief order, then turned his attention to another
corner of the field. From the great tower there was
a wide vista around.

Men lay dead and dying out on the field, yet more
continued to advance—wave upon wave of them
moving towards the castle. Shafts from the long-
bows and bolts from the cross-bows flew back and

forth like deadly hail. The gunner began to prime the cannon, but the very numbers of the attackers enabled them to get close under the tower.

They had chosen their spot cunningly, where an angle of the wall made it impossible for the cannon to be turned on them. It seemed they intended to tie their planks into a rough raft and cross the moat. If that were accomplished they could bring in men with picks and rams to try and mine a way into the base of the tower. Regardless of the danger, Richard leaned over the parapet, quickly summed up the situation and withdrew a split second before an arrow whizzed over.

'Keep firing,' he shouted. 'This may be a ruse for a more concentrated attack elsewhere. I'm going below—'

He saw Alicia then, shot out an arm, grabbed her sleeve and dragged her with him towards the door and the stairs.

'Get below,' he growled, his voice breathless with excitement. 'This is no place for you.'

He almost threw her into the arms of Jenny, who still hovered fearfully close to the stairs, having longed to go down, but feeling unable to desert her mistress.

'We'll be killed if we stay here, my lady,' Jenny urged, hustling her below.

Richard wasted no more time, but having assured himself that Alicia was obeying his instructions and that Jenny would see to it that she went below, he clattered down the stairs ahead of her.

'Oh, my lady—how terrible it all is,' said Jenny. For once Alicia agreed. She allowed herself to be hustled below but it was impossible to withdraw from the action completely; to be cooped up within her chamber would have been unbearable. She ventured into the solar, hoping for a glimpse out of the big oriel window, but that had been shuttered closely to save it from damage.

From outside she could hear the shouting of men—Richard's voice giving an order—the occasional scream as an arrow found its mark. Then came the rumble of heavy stones, of cannon-balls being moved. Alicia left the solar and went down to the great hall.

There lying on the rushes of the floor were the first two casualties. One man had an arrow through his shoulder. Blood spurted from the wound and he moaned incessantly. Alicia ripped off the shirt to examine him and saw that the arrow had gone right through the flesh, its metal head sticking out behind him. Here at least was something she could do to help.

'Jenny—fetch me a saw and some hot water and cloths,' she instructed. 'And bring any herbs or drugs that you can find.'

She had little hope that there would be much of value in the household and chafed that her own collection of medicinal herbs had been left behind at Braister, as they would have proved useful in giving relief to the wounded this day.

Jenny soon returned with the cook's saw and a basin of hot water, clean linen cloths and a box in which were a few dried leaves which Alicia recognised as hemlock, ivy and a piece of mandrake root. Hastily she moistened a little of the hemlock on a piece of linen and applied it to the man's pallid lips, hoping the drug would relieve a little of his pain.

'Courage,' she whispered. 'I'll remove the arrow and dress the wound.'

'Do it—quickly—my lady,' the man urged.

'Help me to hold the arrow steady, Jenny,' Alicia instructed.

Taking a firm grip on the saw, she cut through the shaft so that the pointed metal tip fell. Then with a pull which demanded more strength than gentleness, she withdrew the remainder of the shaft from the man's shoulder. Blood spattered over her gown and dripped from her hands. The man fell back, prostrate. Quickly she rinsed her hands in the bowl of hot water, then taking dry linen made two pads with it and placed one on either side of his shoulder where the hole left by the arrow gaped. She held the pads with a firm pressure to staunch the flow of blood.

'Hold these in place, Jenny,' she instructed.

Jenny obeyed. It was not the first time that mistress and maid had worked together to apply first aid to the injured. Their services had been called upon whenever there was an accident or illness in the household. For all too many things, of course, there was just no cure, death could come in so many different ways, but Alicia, with her love of the wild plants of the countryside, had taken special care to study particularly those which had in the past been known to assist in healing.

Her hands were deft and gentle and she wound the long strips of linen around the man's shoulder to hold the pads close in position. As soon as it was done, she offered him a draught of strong ale.

'Drink it up, it will help with your recovery,' she encouraged.

The man took her hand as she handed him the tankard and kissed her fingers with gratitude.

'You have saved my life, my lady.'

'With God's help, you should recover,' she smiled.

'I—I should try to get back now to help Sir Richard—'

She put a firm hand on his good shoulder to prevent him rising. 'Nonsense. Lie where you are and rest awhile. I doubt if you'll have the strength in that arm to be of much service to anyone for several days.'

She moved over to the second man, but he was already beyond help. Alicia closed the staring eyes, made the sign of the cross and said a prayer for the repose of his soul. As she murmured the words, it seemed natural to add a fervent supplication for the safety of Sir Richard Calder.

What was he doing now, out there on the castle battlements? What was happening in the field below? As if in answer to her unspoken question there came a great shouting—men were running through the great hall, led by de Warante, moving with speed from one vantage-point to another.

'What is it? What is happening?' Alicia called.

'They are trying to cross the moat. They've made a raft and they're bringing up more men behind the cover of some haycarts. It's out of range of the cannon.'

Alicia ran up to the wall walk beside the battlements. A brazier of burning wood was carried out, the men dipped their arrows in hot molten pitch, then after igniting them in the brazier, fired constant showers of arrows down on the cartloads of hay. Before long it began to burn and the men who had been moving behind it fled back until they were out of range.

She looked up at the great tower and caught a

glimpse of Sir Richard. He was ordering his men to
try and loosen some of the huge stones of the
battlements, heaving at them with iron poles. They
struggled, then Richard added his great strength.
Together they pushed the stones over till they fell
down on to the men below who had just begun to
paddle their raft across the moat. There were
screams and yells as the boulders crashed down,
breaking planks and bones and scattering men into
the blood-stained waters of the moat.

Alicia shuddered and returned to the great hall.
She stayed there for the rest of that dreadful day,
doing what she could to staunch the flow of blood
when a wounded man came to her, thankful that
there were not too many of them.

Only when darkness fell was there a lull in the
fighting. By that time Sir Hobart's men had made
one more unsuccessful attempt to cross the moat.
Again they had been forced to retreat, but each
thrust forward left the temporary structure, with
which they were trying to cross the moat, a little
better placed.

A thick mist began to roll in, enveloping first of
all the fetid, stagnant waters of the moat, then
rising upwards so that the countryside around was
shrouded in a thick blanket. Through it the sound
of a trumpet came eerily from the edge of the
woods where Sir Hobart had set up camp.

CHAPTER
SIX

SILENCE descended on the castle. The fighting outside had ceased. It was uncanny after the din and commotion of battle, and those within seemed to hold their breaths, waiting for the next assault. That call of the trumpet had been for the return of Sir Hobart's men, but it could have been a ruse to put them off their guard. Time ticked by.

Men who were near exhaustion from the continual fighting of the day began to assemble in the great hall, leaving only the sentries on guard, as on the previous night. The women servants, continuing their daily tasks as far as possible, managed to produce a quantity of bread, cheese, cold meats and ale. But how long could they hold out? That was the question in everyone's mind—and it was even voiced, whispered, by a few.

'There are so many mouths to feed,' wailed one of the cooks. 'We shall be short of supplies within a few days.'

The tenants who had sought safety from the attackers within the walls of the castle had been able to bring little food with them. Already the countryside had suffered shortages caused by the demands of the armies of both Yorkists and Lancastrians, who pillaged as and where they could. The peasants cared little for the rights or wrongs of either cause, simply trying to stay alive, anxious to get on with their daily tasks. But as bondmen or freemen their fortunes had to be linked to those of their lord, and Sir Richard was reckoned to be better than most.

After eating their fill, men and women lay down on the floor to rest, yet to be in readiness should the alarm be sounded. For those on sentry-duty each watch was kept short, so that they would not relax their vigilance through tiredness. Alicia sat beside one of the men to whom she had been ministering. He had fallen unconscious, but moaned a little now and again. She wiped away the blood that welled up in the corner of his mouth and she chafed that there was little or nothing she could do to help him. Jenny came to her there.

'You should try and get some rest, my lady. I'll sit and watch with this poor soul.'

'I fear he is beyond our help,' Alicia said softly.

'Aye—but please, my lady, you must not tire yourself too much. Who knows what the morrow may bring. Go, lie down, if only for an hour or so.'

There was sense in what Jenny said. Alicia stood up and stretched her cramped limbs.

'Thank you, Jenny. Send for me at once if his condition worsens.'

'That I will.'

Alicia walked slowly, more weary than she had realised, but tired as she was she knew she would be unable to sleep. She turned her steps towards the solar. As she came to the door she heard voices from within—Richard's and the still deeper tones of Brian de Warante. She hesitated for a moment, then softly opened the door and entered. The two men were standing close together in such earnest discourse that they were unaware of her presence.

She had no wish to disturb them, yet she had need of company, for this was one of those occasions when all must stand united—alone, her imagination would all too easily prove host to a riot of horrors. She had sooner face the wrath of the two men than that. She moved quietly and sat on a bench in a dark corner.

'Upon my soul, I know not what to do for the best,' exclaimed Richard. He waved his hands as he spoke in a gesture that seemed to encompass all his pent-up feelings.

'I would not suggest this plan if I believed there might be the remotest chance that help will come from outside,' said de Warante. 'I know you have sent for reinforcements, but who is there who has men at arms to spare just now? You must go to King Edward, speak to him yourself—'

'Would you have me run away?' Richard spoke angrily. ''Twas not for that that you spent so many hours teaching me to shoot a straight arrow or to parry and thrust with my broadsword.'

'Although you are my lord, you are still like a son to me. I respect your courage and your honour, and because of this I bid you leave now. When you are gone I can negotiate an honourable peace—'

'Ha! Hand over my castle and my lands to those swine?'

'Not so, Richard. For the love I bear you, listen to me. 'Tis no easy refuge I am asking you to take. There will be danger enough in getting through the enemy lines unseen. That will call upon all your strength and fortitude—I fear for you, and yet I beg you to take this course.'

Richard began to pace up and down, restlessly.

Alicia thought he must see her, but he kept his eyes down, deep in thought.

'There is sense in what you say, Brian—'

'Indeed there is,' de Warante broke in, seeing his chance of winning Richard to his way of thinking. 'I am convinced there is no chance that reinforcements will arrive unless you can prevail upon the king to act on your behalf.'

'Edward and I were boyhood friends—and I have served him well. I have no doubt he will render me assistance—but I would rather stay and fight. To leave now seems like deserting—'

Alicia heard the ring of repressed excitement in his voice. She remembered that look on his face in the fury of combat earlier in the day.

'What is the sense of that?' de Warante demanded. 'We cannot hold out for more than a week, perhaps two, with great privation, and that will cause terrible hardship to your people. There are women and children here, I know all too well how they will suffer in a long siege and, what is more, I fear they will continue to be repressed if they have to live for ever more under the patronage of those thieving swine. If you stay here, however valiantly you fight, you will be killed in the end. They will have no mercy, for it is in their interest to destroy you completely.'

'That I know—and I would fain make them pay dearly for that privilege—'

'Richard, it is not to save your own life that I bid you leave, dear though that is to me. It is for the sake of us all—for those of your people whose future is in your hands—you have a responsibility to them. Your men have fought for you loyally and well.'

'Aye, they have that.'

'You owe it to them not to continue in the face of such odds. Believe me, if you can win through and get help from the king, there is no greater good you can do.'

Richard stopped his pacing. He strode over to de Warante and grasped him by the shoulders, a gesture of affection.

'You win the argument, Brian. I'll prepare to depart this very evening. I leave in your capable hands the timing and conditions of surrender—' He broke off, choking on the word.

'I shall see that it is an honourable one, Richard. They have no quarrel with me, or with your people, and the sooner this is achieved the sooner they can go about their ordinary tasks to ensure that the crops are tended so that there may be food enough next winter.'

He spoke with such practical sense that Richard had no option but to agree. Alicia too understood exactly why de Warante argued for this course of action—but as she listened and watched, it was as if cold fingers clutched at her heart. De Warante spoke of negotiating a surrender, of handing the castle over to her uncle and Sir Kimball Hobart, and the prospect woke a panic that drained all the blood from her face.

Her uncle would show no mercy. She had suffered many a beating from him and more often from her aunt—Alicia had no doubts as to the fate that now lay ahead of her. Her crime of running away and coming here to Sir Richard Calder would certainly not go unpunished, and she shuddered to think what form their retribution would take. Worst of all was the ultimate horror of that dreaded marriage to Sir Hobart being forced upon her. She leapt to her feet and rushed forward. Both men became aware of her presence and simultaneously turned to face her.

'Oh, my lord,' she cried to Richard. 'Take me with you. I cannot stay here—'

'Alicia!' Richard exclaimed.

Momentarily the men were speechless, neither of them having had any idea that she had been in the room with them, listening. De Warante's eyes searched around the dimly-lit solar as if he feared there might be other eavesdroppers.

'When did you come in here?' he demanded.

'Only a few minutes ago. I—I came only to rest a little—but I could not help overhearing what you were saying, and I implore you, Sir Richard—take me with you.'

'It will be dangerous. The enemy will have patrols about and we could come under fire.'

'I care not. I'd sooner die than be taken again by my uncle.'

'We would have to move with the utmost care—'

'I can be as silent as a mouse. I'll obey your every command—and I can run as swiftly as many a man if I'm put to it,' Alicia cried.

'To take the wench with you will add to your own danger, Richard,' said de Warante.

Alicia blanched. She feared that since de Warante argued against her going there was less likelihood that Richard would take her—and indeed she had no wish to add to his trouble. He seemed to be thinking hard. He strode across the room and back again, then at last he spoke.

'Lady Alicia is right. To leave her here would

place her in great peril.' He paused and looked directly at her. 'If it is truly your choice that you would accompany me, then I'll take you—but think well before you decide.'

'I have no need to think. My mind is made up,' she replied. 'Please, just let me follow you, and I will take my chance.'

'So be it,' said Richard.

De Warante made no further comment. Perhaps he had exhausted his arguments in persuading Richard to take this course of action, and would not risk any word that might unsettle that decision.

'I'm ready when you are,' cried Alicia.

'A few preparations first,' said Richard. 'There's a small boat kept by a door that is almost hidden by a buttress below the great tower—the mist is thick outside—with luck we could punt across the moat—it is dangerous—but it's our only hope. You would travel more safely if you were dressed in your male attire, just as when you came here.'

'Yes, my lord.'

Richard then turned again to de Warante. 'Do you think I should address my men? Advise them of our plan?'

'No, I trust every one of them—and yet, who knows whether there may be a spy in our midst? The fewer that know of your departure the safer for us all.'

'Aye.' Richard heaved a great sigh. 'Then let us make ready to go.'

'My lord, may I confide in my maid?' Alicia asked. 'I would not wish her to think I had deserted her.'

'If you are sure she can be trusted.'

'Of that there is no doubt.'

Alicia sped away to where Jenny remained beside the soldier, only now she knelt at his side.

'He is dead,' she whispered. 'I have prayed for his soul, he just slipped away from this life with no further movement or word.'

Alicia dropped to her knees beside her maid, crossed herself and whispered a brief but fervent prayer.

'Come with me to my bed-chamber,' she said.

She led the way with all possible haste. Jenny followed and as soon as they were alone Alicia turned to her, clasping her hands. 'Jenny—promise you will not repeat what I am about to tell you.'

Jenny's eyes widened in surprise.

'Yes, of course, my lady—you know you can trust me.'

'Sir Richard is escaping from the castle this night and will take me with him. We shall make all possible speed to the king to bring aid to the rest of you.'

Jenny gave a frightened gasp.

'Oh, my lady—do you think that's wise? Think of the dangers out there. How will you get through the enemy lines?'

'That I know not, but we must try. You must stay here, Jenny, and lie low—'

A flicker of relief crossed the maid's face, and Alicia went on, 'Make sure you stay in the servants' quarters. It is unlikely that anyone will question you down there.'

'Don't you worry about me, my lady. Reuben and me will work out some plan—we're well used to looking after ourselves and if it's possible I'll come to you in London.'

Alicia flung her arms around Jenny.

'Bless you. Oh, how I shall miss you. But there's no time to lose. Help me to change my clothes.'

Off came the high headdress, long full overdress, the *cotte*—all rather bloodstained from Alicia's work of ministering to the wounded. On went the brightly coloured hose, the tunic with the padded shoulders, and brief wide skirts that barely covered her buttocks. Her hair was bound tight and covered by a small round cap of the type often worn by page-boys. A wide belt was fastened around her small waist, a sword hanging from it in swashbuckling fashion. Over all went the cloak and hood, fortunately dark in colour, which would help to camouflage her.

Changing took little time. Waiting thereafter seemed endless. It was difficult to sit still, knowing so little of what might lie before her this night. Yet despite her restlessness Alicia felt a strange sense of calm, and wondered at herself that, despite the dangers she would undoubtedly have to face, she was not really frightened. It was with a sense of fatalism that she waited. The knowledge that she would be with Richard gave her courage—he was brave, strong, resourceful, that she knew well. If it was humanly possible to get away from the castle, to evade the enemy and avoid capture, there was no one better equipped than he to do it. But after that? She would be alone with him, in his power even more completely than she was now. That was a disturbing thought. She pushed it from her mind. The immediate dangers were more than enough to be faced. Jenny began to cry softly.

'Oh, my lady! I—I never thought, when we left Braister, that it would come to this.'

'Shh, Jenny,' Alicia consoled her. 'We must

simply hope and pray. But make sure you and Reuben aren't recognised by my uncle or his men. I couldn't bear it if harm befell you.'

A sharp knock came on the door.

For a brief moment Alicia and Jenny clung together, not knowing when—or indeed if ever—they would meet again. There was so much that could have been said and no time for any of it. Alicia kissed her maid.

'God be with you, Jenny—till we meet again.'

'And with you, my lady.'

Then Alicia tore herself from those softly round-ed arms that would have held her a moment longer, and walked to the door. It was Richard himself who waited there, hooded and cloaked.

'Come. We shall go quietly, by the back stair.'

'I am ready,' said Alicia.

Stealthily she followed him down the stone stairs. There was an almost sinister silence in that little-used passageway, deeply recessed within the thickness of the castle wall. Richard moved fast and in trying to keep up with him Alicia almost slipped. She stifled the scream that rose to her throat. Richard stopped momentarily and reached back a hand to grasp hers, gripping with such strength her fingers felt crushed. There was no tenderness in the touch as he guided her down and round the twisting steps.

They were below the great hall now and still going down. The walls were dank, the steps began to feel slippery with moss, the smell of the rank water of the moat, captured and entombed in the narrow walls of the passage, assailed their nostrils. Still they went on down. There seemed to be so many steps that Alicia wondered whether they had not descended below water-level, but at last they reached the bottom.

'Here's the door,' said Sir Richard. 'Stay here while I take a quick look outside.'

The comforting touch of his hand was gone. She heard him fumbling with the heavy bolts on the thick wooden door. They must have been greased in advance, for they slid back almost soundlessly and the door opened without a creak. A swirl of misty air wafted in from the moat—Alicia stood stock still, scarcely daring to breathe. Only a couple of minutes later Richard was back.

'All's clear,' he whispered. 'Give me your hand and tread warily—we're at the edge of the moat, the stones are slippery. We have just to make our way along a short ledge to the boat.'

Without daring to speak, Alicia moved cautiously forward. His hand kept a firm grip on hers and that was indeed necessary, for she could see little. The blackness of the staircase had merely been exchanged for the thick blanket of mist that hung over the moat. Taking each step with care, she moved behind Richard.

'Here's the boat. I'll hand you into it. Sit low on the floor and keep still.'

In the tenseness of the atmosphere it would have been unthinkable to question his commands—and Alicia found herself responding with an obedience that reflected the confidence she felt in his judgment. Even though the floor of the small flat-bottomed boat was wet, she crouched down there, bent almost double. She felt the boat sway as Richard stepped in after her. He had given the little craft a strong push away from the castle walls and they floated out into the mist-covered water, like wraiths.

A moment later she heard the stealthy dip of the paddle. Almost soundlessly Richard began to propel them across the moat. Some instinct told her this was the widest part of that defensive water-way—the enemy had been attacking strongly where the moat was at its narrowest, trying to bridge it. There was less chance of any of Sir Hobart's men guarding or keeping watch on this part of the moat.

Even so, the journey seemed to take a surprisingly long time. Had Richard lost the way in the fog? Was it possible that he was propelling the craft around the castle, instead of straight across the water? Alicia breathed a silent prayer. She dared not speak—voices could have travelled dangerously over the still water. Their progress had to be slow because of the need for silence—but surely they should have been across before now?

A moment later came a light bump. The boat had touched the bank. Alicia lifted her head, only to feel Richard's hand pushing her down again. He stepped out of the boat, tied it to the bank and evidently took a brief reconnoitre before returning to her.

'Get out now,' he whispered, took her hand and helped her on to the walled outer bank of the moat. 'Go over to that clump of trees and wait for me. I have to sink the boat.'

She did as he bade her. As she left, she heard a gurgle of water and guessed that he had pulled the bung from the bottom of the boat to let in the water, thus rendering the small craft useless to the enemy. Doubtless it would sink deep into the mud and mire, quite out of sight, helping to cover their tracks.

The moat at this point was formed naturally by the river—and it was along the river bank that Richard began to lead the way. He moved forward with the surety of someone who really knew where he was going. He had spent much of his boyhood and youth in the vicinity of the castle and the territory was familiar to him. They spoke no word until they had progressed for something like a mile. Then at last Richard paused.

'We're almost at the road that leads to the village,' he said in a low voice. 'There's a bridge over the river and an inn—I know the landlord and shall see if I can get horses. Wait here, it will be safer for me to go there alone.'

'I'll do whatever you say, my lord,' Alicia answered, fearful though she felt. 'But pray do not leave me too long on my own.'

If he heard her last whispered words, he ignored them. Immediately he was gone, and the mist swirled around his departing form, cloaking it as though a fine net curtain had swung back into place.

Alicia peered around cautiously. She was on the edge of a group of trees. She felt the trunk of the one nearest her; it was ancient and gnarled. Wearily she sank down to sit on an outstretched root. An owl hooted eerily deeper in the wood—or was it an owl? How often was that sound used to cover human activity. Was someone there? She tensed— then heard another owl call in answer—followed by an unmistakable flutter of wings. It was indeed a bird. She relaxed a little, yet still her ears strained for any sound of Richard coming back.

Time passed—suppose he never returned? Suppose something had happened to him? The night was full of dangers. Her anxiety grew. She began to feel tense with fear, yet all she could do was to sit and wait—and wait—

It was the horses she heard first, a whinny and a clatter of hooves on gravel. Richard had said there was a road up there. She crouched back in the darkness, pressing her body close against the tree-trunk, pulling her cloak tight around her, allowing her hood to fall forward to shield her face. Was it he—or someone else? She hardly dared to breathe until he spoke her name.

'Alicia.'

At once she darted forward and found him there, leading two horses.

'Mount and be quick,' he whispered impera-tively. 'We must be on our way immediately. Sir Hobart's scouts are higher up along this road, as he fears that reinforcements may be coming to my aid.' He gave a hollow laugh. 'Would that it were true! At the moment the bridge is unguarded. My good friend the landlord has invited the scouts in to take a sup of ale—or maybe something stronger. Put your foot in my hands—'

The upward thrust that he gave her almost threw her into the saddle, then he leapt on to his own steed, gave it a kick with his heels and they were away. Down the road they sped, at full gallop they clattered over the humped-back stone bridge and rode on as fast as their mounts would carry them.

There was a shout from the inn as they fled past, but before the cry could be acted on, it was stifled. Alicia glanced fleetingly back and saw by the light from the doorway a scuffle and a man being drag-ged inside. Then there was no sound but the pound-

ing of their horses' hooves, the snort of their
breath, the creak of harness.

They kept on at speed for about a mile, despite
the mist that added to the danger of keeping to the
road, that made it impossible to see the potholes or
other hazards, relying on the instinct of the horses
to keep them safe. Presently Richard slowed his
mount. As Alicia became aware of this, she reined
in too, until they were walking their horses side by
side.

'We should be safe from pursuit now,' said
Richard. 'The landlord will have dealt with the man
who saw us.'

'Not—?' Alicia breathed, fearful of asking the
question.

'No. He'll merely ply him with liquor till his
memory is too befogged to remember. And he'll
hardly dare to let Sir Hobart know that he was
inside the hostelry when he should have been keeping watch on the bridge. Have no fear, I'll warrant
that for his own sake he'll deny that we ever passed
this way.'

'I cannot see where we are—the mist is so thick.'

''Tis but a few miles along this road to Newgarden. It has a good hostelry where we may stay
the night. We should be there within the hour.'

Alicia glanced fearfully about her and kept close
to Richard. 'Do you not fear robbers?'

''Tis always well to keep a lookout,' he agreed.
'But the outlaws do not usually frequent this stretch
of road; they prefer the open heath beyond Newgarden, where there's cover in the scrub. I wouldn't
wish to ride that stretch of road at this hour. Come,
let's hurry.'

Again they both urged their horses to a quicker

pace. They met no other travellers and, as he had
predicted, about an hour later a cluster of lights
ahead told them they were nearing the market town
of Newgarden. The road led straight into it and a
short distance along was the hostelry that Richard
was seeking, the Green Man.

As they clattered into the inner courtyard, an
ostler came out of the stables to take their horses
from them. Richard gave him instructions that their
mounts were to be well looked after, for they would
be required to carry them on another long journey
the following day. Then he strode towards the inn
door. Just before entering, he turned and spoke to
Alicia, keeping his voice low, his face so close to
hers that she could feel his breath warm and sweet
on her cheek.

'We're not yet so far from Leet that we can feel
safe. For one more day at least you'll have to ape
the part of a boy, for I daren't ask here for female
attire for you—it would arouse too much notice and
suspicion.'

'I am perfectly prepared to continue in this role,
my lord,' she replied.

'Then we must both take care to remember that
you are my squire. So, when we are not alone, I
shall call you—', he paused to consider a moment.
'How about Amandus?'

'I do not know this name, Sir Richard.'

' 'Tis one that comes back to me from my studies
of Latin. One day I'll tell you its meaning.'

'It will serve as well as any other name, surely,
until I can safely resume my own,' she said.

'Then, Amandus—let us see what food and
accommodation mine host can offer to two weary
travellers.'

Never before had Alicia travelled so far that the journey had necessitated staying at an inn. She was accustomed to moving from manor to manor in the customary way of rich households who, when they had exhausted the stores and supplies of one domain, found the easiest and cheapest method of living was to move on to the next. That was a simple economic fact, but those journeys with Aunt Margaret and Uncle Rufus and their retinue could always be made within one day. It was therefore with some trepidation as well as curiosity that she followed Richard into the stuffy warmth of the inn.

The room was low-ceilinged, the atmosphere close, a log fire blazed in the wide hearth and some half a dozen men sat about resting, talking, drinking frothing tankards of ale. Two were at a long table, eating meat and bread. Richard seated himself beside them and Alicia took her cue from him and settled herself there too. The landlord hurried forward.

'Meat for two hungry travellers,' ordered Sir Richard. 'And ale, bread, cheese, a pie—anything you've got that's fit for gentlemen to eat.'

'Yes, my lord—certainly—'

The landlord, recognising quality when he saw it, bustled out to send in a serving-wench with the best that his kitchens could offer.

'And a room for the night,' added Sir Richard. 'Tell them to get the best they have ready—and see that the bed's well aired, or I'll have them thrown in the duck-pond.'

'I've a fine room. I'll send up straight away and have the fire lit and clean sheets put on the bed—'

Alicia sat silently, staring at the table and not daring to raise her eyes to look at her companion.

Her heart beat so fast that she felt it might choke her—there was no other way possible, she knew that. It would have been unthinkable for Richard to ask for two separate rooms. Even to have a room for the two of them was rather unusual, for men were mostly expected to sleep together in dormitory-like accommodation.

There was no way out of it. She would be compelled to spend the night alone with him, in that bedroom which was even now being prepared for them—but just what would he expect of her? She quailed at the thought.

'Eat up. Aren't you hungry, boy?' he asked.

She started, having been scarcely aware that the food had been placed before her.

'I—I think perhaps I'm too weary to eat, sire.'

For some reason that made him laugh. She had seized on it as an excuse that might allow her to keep some privacy this night.

'You seemed alert enough when we rode in here,' he commented drily. 'Eat up and take a sup of ale—'twill make a man of you—perhaps.'

Alicia gave him a wry smile. It was all very well for him to be amused at her predicament, but everything she did seemed only to compromise her more and more. She took a sip of ale to moisten her dry lips, but she was not accustomed to such a strong brew and hesitated to take much in case her head became fuddled.

Perhaps the worst thing of all was that Richard seemed to be thoroughly enjoying the situation and she could see no way out of it. After his meal—and Richard had done justice to the cold roast beef, bread and pickles that had been set before them— he had drunk a bowl of soup, quaffed a quart of ale and finished off with a juicy apple, then leaned back in his chair, looked smugly satisfied, stretched, and yawned.

'We've a long journey tomorrow, Amandus,' he said. 'Let us away to our bed. We'll need all the rest we can get if we're to make good time to London.'

Alicia swallowed. The moment had arrived.

'I—I—yes, my lord—'

It could not be put off any longer. She rose and followed Sir Richard up the stairs and into the room which had been allotted to them.

As the innkeeper had promised, a fire had been lit and already it had warmed the room, in the centre of which stood a large four-poster bed. It was fashioned of dark and light timbers with a heavy carved headpiece and a canopy of painted cloth, a cheaper substitute for tapestry, and woven curtains. It was a bed of considerable luxury for such a hostelry and it dominated the room completely. There was no way of ignoring the presence of that great double bed.

Sir Richard, as befitted his superior status of lord and master, strode ahead of her into the room. He pressed his hand on to the bed-covers, testing the softness of the feather-bed beneath and seemed satisfied. Alicia remained in the doorway, her eyes downcast and her heart beating like a caged bird within her breast. Richard turned, with his back to the fire and looked at her.

'Well—come in, Amandus. Shut the door and keep the heat in.'

Alicia obeyed but still she stood, with her back to the closed door, keeping her distance.

'Are you going to stay over there all night? You'll

be stiff with cold in the morning. Come over by the fire.'

Slowly Alicia moved towards him, her head lowered, unable to lift her eyes and look straight at him. Last evening he had spoken of them spending some time together—this night it seemed as if that would be forced upon them, and in this compromising situation she was completely at his mercy.

She sensed rather than saw him move forward. A moment later her hand was imprisoned in his and firmly she was drawn towards the fire and towards—him. She felt the warmth of the one no less palpably than she was conscious of the magnetism and vitality of the other.

The pressure of his fingers on her hand seemed to send a spark of life thrilling through her. She had to lift her eyes and the look that she saw in his was so disturbing that she opened her mouth to utter a small gasp.

Immediately his arms closed tight around her, her body was crushed against his and his mouth claimed hers. The pressure of those possessive lips spoke more eloquently than any words they could have uttered—there was magic in their movement over her mouth. She closed her eyes, almost swooning with the response that leapt from her lips as they clung to his kiss. His hands moved with firm caressing strength, circling the slenderness of her waist, till she seemed to be almost lifted from her feet, as her whole physical being strained with its desire to become wholly a part of him.

Time seemed to stand still as she remained clasped in that embrace. All conscious thought was overruled and the passion that took possession of her seemed to blot out both mind and soul. Never in her wildest dreams had she imagined that she could feel like this—so separate from all she had been taught, from all her understanding of life—and yet so very, very, much more alive than she had ever been.

She made a small movement as reality began to creep back and her conscience leapt quivering to admonish her for such wanton conduct. But the movement seemed only to move her body against Richard's in a way that made her even more aware of his manliness. It seemed also to rouse him to even more demanding passion. Her breasts tingled with delight as they discovered the pressure of his chest, rock-hard, muscular—he had loosed his leather tunic and shirt so that she could smell and feel the sweet warmth of his skin.

The desire that leapt in her was almost impossible to deny, its power rooted deep in the urgency of creation. Yet even as she seemed to be drowning in a hunger of love, her conscience roused itself once more, making it impossible for her to push aside completely the years of civilised teaching, of social behaviour, of a sense of right and wrong, deeply implanted by both church and home. It jolted her sharply back to reason.

She wrenched her mouth away from his, lifted her hands so that his chest was thrust back from contact with her firm young breasts. At first she thought he was not going to release her. Then as he continued to keep his arms around her, even tightened their grip momentarily, she cried out in her alarm.

'No—no! Let me go.'

The sound of her voice, although not over loud, broke through the spell. It conveyed to Richard more definitely than her struggling had done that she was becoming distressed. At once he loosened his hold on her, though he did not fully release her.

'Sire—you have no right to treat me so,' said Alicia.

A slight smile lifted one corner of his mouth.

'My lady—I had not realised that you were—objecting. For my part, I felt such pleasure in kissing you that I would fain continue the occupation—'

He made as if he would have tightened his arms around her again.

'No,' she cried, taking a quick step back from him. He raised his eyebrows and regarded her with a mocking smile.

'No? That wasn't the message I read from the soft touch of your lips, Amandus.'

'It—it is not right.'

'Ah, but who is to say what is right? I certainly can feel no wrong in such a sweet sensation.'

'It is not for us to question the teaching that we have been given in these matters.'

''Tis but the teaching of men. I hold my own standards of right and wrong.'

'Perhaps for you it's different, sire—but for myself—'

'Yes?'

Her voice had trailed off. He waited and then, as she made no answer, still struggling to find the right words, he added, softly—'Can something so pleasurable truly be wrong?'

'Oh yes, sire.' That was easy to answer. 'I have found that most of the pleasurable things are considered wrong.'

He chuckled.

'So—you are not denying that it is pleasurable. Then, let us repeat the pleasure—'

He stepped forward and would have taken her back into his arms, but she side-stepped hastily. She dared not allow that disturbing contact with him to recur.

'No!'

This time she was so filled with horror and guilt that her voice rose slightly on a note of panic. She ran to the opposite side of the room.

'Please—please, sire—leave me be. I will not be bedded before I am wedded.'

His brows drew down over his eyes in a frown that made it impossible in that dim candle-light for her to read the expression on his face. He made no attempt to follow her across the room, but turned his back on her and looked down into the fire. Alicia stayed with her back pressed hard against the wood of the door, as if she hoped to gain some strength from its solidity. Her heart beat fast beneath the boy's tunic. Wide-eyed she gazed across the room to where Sir Richard stood staring into the blaze.

If he was determined to force her there was no way she could resist; she was physically as weak as a kitten in comparison to him, but she was sure she was right and pride came to her aid in her determination not to give in easily.

Richard stood there some minutes, as if making a great effort at self-control. Then abruptly he stepped to one side, turned to look directly at her and she saw the cold, hard expression on his face, the glint of anger in his eyes.

'My lady—I have no wish to force myself upon you. That is something I have never done to any

woman, and I assure you I have not the least
intention of doing so now. You are as safe in this
room, alone with me, as you would be in your
virginal bed at Braister.'

She had drawn herself up proudly to show that
she was not to be treated lightly and stood with her
head held defiantly high. Perhaps she had been at
fault for not repulsing him sooner. She cursed the
weakness of her own body that had allowed her to
seem at first to accept his love-making. Now that
her sense of duty and propriety had reasserted
itself, she was sorry that he should be angry at being
repulsed, but she dared not make any overture that
would soften the tension. She was too well aware
that the passion that lay unspent between them
could so easily be re-ignited.

With a gesture, sardonic in its flamboyance, he
gave her a mocking bow and moved aside from the
fireplace, then indicated that she should move
nearer the warmth.

'You have my word, and it is that of a knight and
a gentleman—that I shall stay only in this small
corner of the room, till daybreak.'

To emphasise his point, he squatted down on the
rushes of the floor, well to the side of the fire, as far
as possible from the great bed.

'It shall be as if it had a ten-foot wall around it.
All the rest of the room and its accoutrements are at
your disposal.'

Still she hesitated. After a brief pause he spoke
again, and there was a note of impatience in his
voice.

'What more reassurance do you need, my lady?
It is essential that we both settle ourselves to rest
this night so as to be in readiness and fresh for the

long journey tomorrow. Goodnight, Amandus.'

That name again. He had said that some day he would tell her what it meant—for now, she could merely answer to it.

'Goodnight, Sir Richard.'

Without undressing, she lay down on the huge feather-bed and covered herself with the sheets and blankets.

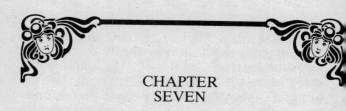

CHAPTER
SEVEN

WHEN Alicia awoke the next morning the light of
the new day was filtering in through the low window
of the bed-chamber. With a start she realised where
she was, sat up and looked anxiously towards the
shadowy corner where Richard had declared he
would spent the night. He was not there. Her eyes
darted round the room, peering into the dimness.
She was alone.

She threw back the covers and leapt out of bed.
A ewer and bowl stood on a chest by the window,
where she washed her face and hands and had just
dried them on a rough linen towel when the door
opened and in came Sir Richard.

'Good. You're up,' he said. His voice was curt
and clipped, his face unsmiling. 'There's breakfast
below. Waste no time—I would be on the road as
early as possible.'

'Yes, my lord.'

His urgency was infectious. She belted on her
sword, her fingers so agitated that they grew clumsy
and it took her longer to fix the fastening than she
would have wished. Sir Richard watched her but
offered no assistance. Downstairs men still slept on
the hard benches by the fire. On a corner of a table
stood a loaf of bread, a dish of butter, a platter
with salt herrings, one jug of ale and another of
milk.

'Eat well. We've a long day ahead,' Richard instructed.

Obediently Alicia drank some milk, tore a piece from the loaf, spread it with butter and placed a piece of salt fish on it. It was strong but tasty. Mindful of the need to hurry she took only enough to give her sustenance and was soon ready to follow Richard out to where the horses waited.

The sun was rising in a glorious orb of gold as they clattered out of the yard of the inn and set off at a trot through the sleeping town. All trace of last night's mist had vanished. Soon they had left Newgarden behind them and came to the heath. The horses were fresh, eager to go, and needed little urging to set off at a canter through the dewy morning.

The air was sweet with the scent of gorse-blossom, birds sang in the thickets of blackthorn and bramble, rabbits scurried away, their white scuts bobbing. Clumps of fir-trees made a dark distant backcloth, but no trees were permitted to grow close to the road as a precaution against outlaws who might hide behind them, waiting to attack innocent travellers. The ancient track led straight across the wide flat heath, then dropped down slightly into a vale that was richly cultivated and more wooded. The tender green of foliage of beech and oak enhanced the beauty of the spring day.

Soon Richard had drawn slightly ahead of her, and although Alicia urged her horse to greater speed it was impossible to keep up with him. After a while she gave up trying and simply settled to an enjoyment of the ride. On such a morning it was impossible not to feel how good it was to be alive, to delight in the breeze whistling past, blowing their cloaks out behind. Action such as this seldom came the way of girls; never before had she experienced such freedom and her ebullient youthfulness revelled in it.

It was true that Richard had this morning treated her with a curt remoteness, and she could not be unaware that it would have been different between them had she consented last night to become his paramour. He had not so much as touched her hand, given her one gentle look or spoken a soft word since then. Indeed she suspected he was harbouring a smouldering resentment at her rejection of his advances—but for how long would that situation hold? Where would they stay this night—and the next?

She hated this chasm that had grown between them, but if she attempted to bridge it would it again awaken that powerful, almost uncontrollable, sensual urge? She longed for a demonstration of friendship but dared make no overture towards it. Her lips quivered as she remembered the joy Richard's kisses had awakened in her whole body. She had been warned of the lusts of the flesh and the downfall it could bring to give way to such passion—it had been easy to accept those admonitions humbly before she had experienced that rapture that Richard had aroused in her. Somehow she must avoid any situation which might lead to a repetition of last night's amorous episode. Then she chided herself for allowing her thoughts to ramble so wildly. One glance at Richard's face this morning should have told her she had nothing to fear from him. He was so distant that she truly felt he had scarcely given her a thought. Far from showing any sign that he was enjoying her company in any way, he made it obvious she was but an encumbrance to him.

In the course of the morning they covered something like ten miles. At midday they stopped to rest their horses and themselves and ate bread and cheese, but Richard was anxious to move on again as soon as possible. They had been riding again for less than an hour when his horse stumbled. It did not fall, but it began to slow. It was limping. He reined in, dismounted and lifted the horse's hoof. Alicia sat her horse close by, watching.

'What is it?'

'Probably pulled a ligament. It's these cursed rough roads.'

He ran a hand down the foreleg. The horse stood with its weight on the other legs—obviously Richard could no longer ride it.

'Luckily we made good time early in the day,' he said. 'We haven't too far to go now. I'll walk.'

He strode along, leading his injured mount, whilst Alicia rode at his side. She was relieved to find that he now seemed to be in a more relaxed and cheerful mood and he began to ply her with questions about herself, asking about her childhood and her family.

'My parents both died of the pestilence when I was about fourteen,' she said. 'I wasn't living at home at that time, having been boarded out in the household of my lord Harleston.'

Sir Richard understood that perfectly. It was the custom for all families to send their children to the households of others from the age of about eight until they grew up. This was said to make sure that the children learnt good manners, but in reality it was hoped they might meet some rich patron or great lord, whose influence would give them material benefits and perhaps lead to an advantageous marriage.

'So it was for me,' said Richard. 'I spent all my youth in the household of Richard, Duke of York.'

'That turncoat!' Alicia exclaimed. 'He who for years acted as one of the king's advisers and then took up arms against him?'

'Henry was no longer fit to be king,' Richard retorted.

'My father, God rest his soul, always spoke of King Henry as a gentle learned man.'

'Gentle he may have been, and something of a scholar, but those were not the qualities needed for a ruler; besides it's well known that Henry is subject to bouts of insanity.'

'I don't think it's right to imprison him in the Tower,' Alicia said staunchly.

'Surely you wouldn't wish the country to be governed by a lunatic?'

'He had a capable wife in Queen Margaret.'

'She made the man into a puppet. It was never Henry who ruled. And she never forgot that she was French. She's over there now, plotting no doubt to try and launch a new attack on this country.'

'There are plenty will rally to her, when she comes,' Alicia said. 'She fights for the right of her son to inherit the throne—you must admit his claim is a valid one?'

'Rubbish. He's but a child. How can he rule? That was part of the trouble in the past. Henry was only eight months old when his father, Henry the Fifth, died. While the young king was growing up, the country was governed by a succession of power-mad men who thought only to better themselves.'

'Such as the Duke of York,' Alicia pointed out wickedly.

'God rest his soul,' muttered Richard. 'Your mind has been well poisoned by those Lancastrians you lived with. Edward will make a good ruler, I am sure of that. He's a direct descendant of Edward the Third and he grows more kinglike every time I see him.'

Curiosity began to overcome her instilled dislike of anyone who followed the cause of the white rose.

'You know him well, I suppose, since he is the son of the Duke of York, who was your patron?'

'We passed much of our youth together. I am some four years older than Edward, so it often fell to me to look after him and we became close friends.'

Alicia could not help being a little impressed that Richard was familiar with the new young king.

'What is he like?'

'He's a giant of a man. Stands six feet three inches tall—and 'tis said he's one of the handsomest young men in the kingdom. Besides, he's a stalwart fighter.'

'Fighting! That's all you knights think about. Tell me something about him as a man. I've heard that the Earl of Warwick is seeking to marry him to a French princess?'

'Huh!' Richard discounted that idea abruptly. 'Edward is a man who makes up his own mind. You can take my word for it—he won't allow Warwick or anyone else to choose a wife for him.'

She was surprised at the decisiveness with which Richard spoke. 'I thought these things were always arranged and that kings and queens had little say when it came to marriage.'

'Perhaps that is usually so, but I know it'll be different with Edward.'

'You really do like and admire him, don't you?'

'Oh yes. I've fought with him in many a battle. I was with him when he had to flee to Calais, but I knew it wouldn't be long before we returned. And so it was. I'll never forget that triumphant march after we landed again on English soil. Warwick was in command, we were only two thousand—but men flocked to join us. By the time we reached London we had over twenty thousand with us. Ah! Those were stirring times.'

'And there were more battles, more men killed and wounded,' Alicia said. 'It would have been better for England if Edward had stayed in Calais.'

He glanced at her sharply, his face hard.

'You understand naught of these matters. Margaret was marching south with her rabble—and do you know what she had promised them?'

Alicia shook her head.

'She had no money to pay them, so you can imagine what sort of men made up her army and she promised them unbridled plunder, pillage and rape in the southern counties!'

Alicia shuddered. The picture he drew was too horrible to contemplate.

'That had to be stopped—and we did it.' Richard's eyes shone with remembered excitement. 'We didn't stay in London. We marched north and joined battle with them at Northampton. I remember it was pouring with rain and Henry couldn't even keep his powder dry. He couldn't use his artillery—'

He broke off with a merry laugh, but she saw no pleasure in it.

'I've had enough of fighting and death and destruction.'

'There are times when battles have to be fought and won.'

'You were victorious at Northampton, but it was a different story at Wakefield,' Alicia could not resist pointing out.

'That was a sad day. The Duke of York himself was slain there and to parade his death, his head was displayed on a pike above the city gates. They even made a paper crown for his head because he had been named as heir to the king.'

'How horrible!'

'There's been too much blood spilled over this great land of ours. What we desperately need now is a period of peace and firm government.'

'If only it could be so,' sighed Alicia. 'But how will it end? These so-called Wars of the Roses have been going on for ten years now.'

'That no one can say—but I fear it will drag on for some time yet. How can it be otherwise when ill-informed people such as you would welcome the return of Henry.' His voice was angry and bitter.

'I could say equally—when people like you keep that usurper Edward on the throne—'

'And that shows your Lancastrian ignorance!' he snapped. 'I tell you Edward will make a much better king than ever Henry did. He could bring this country to peace and prosperity if only your friends of the red rose will leave him to get on with governing.'

His words incensed Alicia, made her deeply aware of the depth of distrust and hatred that could spring up from their being attached to different sides in this appalling civil war. He walked on beside her in silence for several minutes and seemed to be deep in thought.

They negotiated a particularly rough piece of road where a pothole was so large that it flooded right across the old track, making it necessary for them to make a small loop, as obviously many other travellers on this much-used highway had done before them. Then Richard caught hold of her horse's bridle and halted her.

'I've had enough of walking. I'll share your mount for the rest of this day's journey,' he said. 'Take your feet out of the stirrups and move forward.'

He gave her no option but to obey, and lithely he swung himself up behind her. His arms closed tightly round her so that he lifted her a little as he settled himself into the saddle, then drew her down and she found herself seated almost on his lap.

He clicked his tongue, telling the horse to move forward, and Alicia was acutely conscious of the pressure of the muscles of Richard's thighs which every step of the horse made into a disturbingly sensual movement. His arms held her on either side, as he grasped the reins. She was shy and embarrassed by such continual physical contact, and kept her eyes lowered and fixed on the bobbing neck and mane of the horse. Richard gave no sign that he found such proximity in any way disturbing and he encouraged the animal to break into a gentle trot. He was leading his own mount and watched its gait with concern.

'I think this speed will do no harm to either animal,' he observed.

Alicia made no reply and they travelled in silence for a short time. Then again he began to question her.

'You still have not told me much of your life. How did you fare, Alicia? There was a time when I thought you were a sweet and biddable maiden—but more recently I've discovered you have a strong will of your own.'

Just what did he mean by that? Seated in front of him, astride the horse, it was impossible to look at him and she had an uncomfortable feeling that if she could have seen his face she would only find that mocking expression which she had come to know so well. She tossed her head, then answered seriously, almost primly.

'I did my best to be good. Indeed I still do—but I must admit it does not come easily to me.'

He gave a soft laugh.

'You said last night that you found most pleasurable things were considered wrong.'

She did not wish to be reminded of that, especially at this moment when every part of her seemed to be enfolded, held, touched by him—when she was once again so vulnerable. Deliberately she sought for words that might help to cool this heady, hot feeling that he had aroused.

'One thing that I did not find too hard was to apply myself to my lessons,' she said.

'You have learnt to read and write?'

'Oh yes—I was the only child of my parents, and although I know my father dearly wished that I had been a boy, he loved me truly. He made me take lessons with our chaplain when I was a small child, and sometimes my father taught me himself. I think he was loath to send me away, for I was almost ten when I first went to my lord Harleston's household. By that time I could read and write passably well, and I haven't forgotten. Indeed I really enjoy reading and I wrote to my parents as often as any messenger might be able to take a letter for me.'

'Were you happy in the Harlestons' household?'

'Alas, I fear not. I grieved sadly for my father in particular, who had always been so good and kind to me. But I was kept very busy, and I believe I learned well. I can take charge of a household if need be and keep the accounts, and I have a book well filled with receipts and prescriptions for the making of lotions and unguents.'

'I noticed you have some knowledge of medicine, and I haven't yet properly thanked you for taking care of my men who were wounded in battle.'

'There was little I could do for them, but my mistress Harleston was a wise woman when it came to medicines, and this I always found interesting.'

'You were gathering herbs that first day I met you in the woods by Braister Castle, weren't you?'

'When I see a rare plant, I usually gather it, for often they have good uses. The day we met I'd escaped simply to be on my own.'

Alicia's mind slipped back to that fine day, not so long ago. What ever the future might bring—and she hardly dared think what might lie ahead—that chance meeting with Richard had changed her life for ever.

'Tell me about your parents?' Sir Richard asked.

'My father was Lord Clement Bartolf and my mother the daughter of the Earl of St Albans.'

Both had been rich and influential and she was

proud to name them. Had she been a boy there
would have been a great inheritance, but, as it was,
all the property had gone to her uncle, her mother's
brother, Rufus Blount.

'Ah! I've heard of both families. They were
noble people.'

'May God rest their souls.'

'Amen.'

'After my parents died, my uncle and aunt
Blount sent for me.'

'And you have lived with them since then?'

'That is so. I suppose they felt no obligation to
put me out to any other household. I did once ask to
be sent back to the Harlestons, but Aunt Margaret
wouldn't hear of it.'

'Did that surprise you, Alicia?'

'Not entirely. I believe my aunt found me useful.
I must admit she took great pains to teach me her
way of administering the household. As a man, you
may not be aware of just what that involves.'

'It is not something I have given much thought
to,' he said with a slight smile. 'Though I always
find it a charming sight to see the womenfolk at
their spinning-wheels.'

'Charming it may look, but it is quite hard work,
I assure you, sire,' she said with asperity. 'Especially when it is necessary to provide the whole household with new sheets or blankets.'

'I can well believe it.'

'Perhaps more important are those other items,
of making sure that the larders are well stocked
before winter comes, that the hams are properly
cured, the meat well salted, that the vegetable
garden is well tended, that there's a plentiful supply
of wine and beer laid down, as well as making all

those day-to-day items of butter and cheese and bread and pastries and seeing that the stocks of poultry are kept up and that the pigeons are breeding well. You're so accustomed to living in well-ordered households that you probably have no idea what it means if some store goes mouldy and is uneatable just when you need it and there's no means of replacing it for months to come.'

'Then it's the time to move on to the next manor, if you have one,' Sir Richard commented with a merry laugh.

'But when there's snow on the ground, as all too often happens, that isn't a good time to move house,' Alicia pointed out.

'And you've learnt all this?' he said.

She thought she detected again that note of mockery in his voice.

'I'm sorry if it sounds dull to you,' she replied sharply.

' 'Tis a pity you have no cure for this affliction of my horse.'

'If I had I would have applied it long ago. I certainly have no desire to lengthen the time of our journey.'

Since her back was to him she could not see his face, but he tightened his grip round her slender frame as if he was angered and wanted to hurt her. The strength of his grip reminded her of the physical power of the man, and she blanched. She had been a fool to have spoken so, for she was entirely at his mercy—and yet there was something about him that continually needled her into reckless provocation. Her uncle would have hit her for making such a rash comment. She began to think she should voice some discreet apology, even though she did not really mean it. When Richard spoke, however, his voice was coolly even.

'We are now not far from the house of my lord Clifton. Do you know of him?'

'I believe I've heard my father mention his name, but I don't think the Cliftons were acquaintances of my uncle.'

'They would know one another well enough, but they wouldn't be allied in the same causes. Cedric Clifton is a loyal Yorkist and he has in the past been a good friend to me. I propose to seek his hospitality for this night.'

Alicia was relieved to learn that they would not be staying at an inn—but would that mean she would not again be put into the position of sharing a room with Richard?

With some trepidation she asked—'Will you tell him who I am?'

She held her breath, waiting for his reply, and when it came his voice was so cool it chilled her.

'My lady—you worry too much about your virtue.'

'I—I merely wished to know if—if I have still to play the boy—'

'Oh, don't prevaricate. You are as transparent as a pool of clear water. You are fretting yourself because you have no wish to share a room with me this night.'

'Since you know my thoughts, why do you ask?'

She heard him draw his breath in sharply.

'I assure you that that desire is mutual. I shall announce you immediately as the daughter of Lord Clement Bartolf and I feel sure that Lord and Lady Clifton will make arrangements that will allow you to sleep this night with your maidenhood unsullied by any rough male presence.'

She made no answer. His tongue had a cutting edge that she had no wish to provoke further. They spoke not another word, though they rode so close on the back of the one horse that she could feel Richard's warm breath on the nape of her neck. His arms still imprisoned her and their thighs were in constant contact, rocked by the rhythmic movement of the horse.

The house of Lord Clifton was newly built in a Gothic style. It was long, low and rambling with no turrets or battlements, but had many wide windows set in its façade. It had been constructed in the modern manner with more attention to comfort than to defence, but entry was still made by a drawbridge over a moat. This led to an outer courtyard.

Sir Richard was soon recognised as a welcome visitor. Quickly he gave instructions for the care of his lamed horse to a groom who led the injured animal away. Then Richard moved towards the house and strode along to the great hall. Alicia followed at a discreet distance.

Lord Clifton was but a little older than Richard himself and the two men greeted each other with warm handshakes. Lady Clifton too seemed to be delighted to welcome her visitor. She was rather short and heavily pregnant and had a kindly smiling face. Alicia stayed slightly behind Sir Richard as he greeted his old friends, but almost immediately he drew her into the company and explained her presence and identity.

'You are most welcome, Lady Alicia,' said Lord Clifton. 'I believe my father was well acquainted with Lord Bartolf. Indeed as a boy I have vivid recollection of him at a hunting-party on our estate in Ware.'

'I am delighted to make your acquaintance,' said Alicia. She was not quite sure whether to bow or to curtsy, and made an obeisance that was somewhere between the two. 'I must apologise for my strange garb, but it was necessary for our escape from Leet.'

Lady Clifton came forward to greet Alicia with a welcoming kiss on her cheek. She stood a mere four feet six inches tall, a head shorter than Alicia.

'I would offer you some feminine garments, but I fear they would never fit you.'

''Tis no matter,' Alicia assured her easily. 'I've grown accustomed to being clad thus and doubtless it'll be better for me to remain so now, until we reach London.'

Lady Clifton chatted easily and in such a friendly fashion that they might have known each other for many years instead of only a few hours. For the most part they left the men to talk together—but there was one piece of their conversation that came to Alicia, even as she half-listened to Lady Clifton. Cedric Clifton was talking and he mentioned a name.

'They tell me that the Lady Elizabeth—'

Perhaps it was the rapid hush with which Richard silenced him that made the words penetrate more. For some reason Alicia was certain they were referring to the same lady who had been at Leet and, while not wishing to appear to listen, she found herself hanging on their words.

'The lady is quite beautiful, is she not?' asked Lord Clifton.

'Aye, she is indeed,' Richard replied. 'It had been arranged that she should remain at Leet until such time—'

He broke off and it seemed to Alicia that there was an infinite sadness in the way he shook his head.

Lord Clifton nodded as if he understood perfectly. Then Richard continued, 'I had news that the attack on Leet was imminent, so felt it imperative to arrange for her departure immediately. Did she reach here safely?'

'She did, God be praised. And it was from her that I learned of your predicament. I would have brought men to assist you, Richard, but I knew that you would first of all wish me to see to the lady's safety.'

'You did well.'

'I conducted her to London myself. Rest assured she is in no danger at the present time. And the wedding—?'

'Arranged some time ago,' Richard replied solemnly.

'And I can never thank you enough for your help.'

The two men had been talking in low tones and Alicia had only just been able to catch the gist of their conversation, but one thing was crystal clear—they were talking about that beautiful lady who had been at Richard's fireside the night that Alicia arrived at Leet. She had left the following morning and Richard had spared men he could ill afford to lose in order to make sure that she had a safe journey. Evidently she too had passed a night here in the Cliftons' manor house and now, once again, Richard's concern was centred on assuring himself of that other woman's safety. And what was this talk of a marriage? Alicia felt a sickness in the pit of her stomach.

'Are you all right?'

Lady Clifton's voice penetrated her thoughts, and Alicia realised that she was looking at her curiously and that she had not been paying the least attention to her conversation.

'I'm sorry. I'm a little tired after the journey,' she apologised with a wry smile.

The meal and the evening passed almost in a dream. She made a conscious effort to be polite and to appear relaxed, to put that puzzling conversation from her mind, but for some reason she did not find it easy. Every now and again the image of that beautiful face seemed to dance before her eyes taunting her. But why should she care so much? True, when she had first met Sir Richard, she had found him attractive. Looking back on it she tried to tell herself that it had been mostly a desire to escape from marriage with Sir Hobart Kimball that had driven her to leave Braister, but in her heart she knew there had been an even more powerful reason. She had sought—well, she hardly knew what—but something more than the brief dalliance that Richard would have enjoyed.

He found her desirable, that she knew. She could not easily forget the flaring of passion that had sprung into life between them last night. He would have shared the bed with her had she been willing— but that had little to do with love and less with marriage.

As they talked when they travelled together, with Richard walking his lamed horse, their differences had been more apparent than any accord.

She winced as she remembered several aspects of that conversation. Yet she could not dismiss him from her thoughts. Every day she passed in his company made her more intensely aware of him. He was a man that no one could ignore. If only he had a higher regard for her—but there was no question of that, his affections were already captured by that other woman. Elizabeth. Elizabeth who? She longed to ask, but dared not.

Again the next morning they were on their way almost as soon as dawn lightened the sky.

'We must travel fast today, to make up for the time we lost yesterday,' Richard said tersely. 'I wish to be in London by well before dark.'

Alicia had slept soundly and felt much refreshed, and again she spurred her horse on, determined to keep pace with him. They met and overtook more travellers than they had done the previous day, though the condition of the road was just as bad. This made it particularly difficult for the carriers and other carts, and once they passed a group of people clustered, shouting and gesticulating, round a cart stuck up to its axle in mud.

On and on they rode and with fresh horses they covered the ground swiftly. Richard glanced back occasionally to make sure that Alicia was not falling too far behind, but that was the only concession he gave her. There was no opportunity for conversation until midday, when they stopped at an inn. The rest was welcome to Alicia. She was glad to dismount and to partake of the bread, cheese and ale that the landlord brought them, but she was in no mood for pleasantries and Richard too ate in silence, until all too soon he rose to his feet again.

'It's time to ride on, Alicia,' he announced.

'Have we far to go?'

'No. Two hours more and we should be in London.'

Once they were through the city gates the streets seemed to close in on them, the houses shutting out almost all the sunlight with their overhanging upper stories. Alicia looked round with excitement and interest. It was many years since she had been to the capital and then she had been but a child so she could scarcely remember it. Dwellings and business premises elbowed close to each other—drapers, spice merchants, furriers, barbers and every other trade. Not only were the narrow streets alive with people, rich and beggarly, and with horses, carts, litters and people carrying bundles and bags, but the roads themselves were covered in filth of every sort and the stench was an affront to the nose.

'Keep close to me,' Richard ordered.

He rode slowly now, so that she could keep right on his tail, past a market and a church and innumerable hostelries and on until they came to a street that was a little quieter than the rest. It seemed to have several large houses. He led the way down an alley. Alicia followed, and behind the houses they came to a yard at one side of which was a row of stables. Richard reined in, swung himself out of the saddle and came towards Alicia.

'Where are we?' Alicia asked.

'Home,' he replied tersely.

He held up his arms to catch her as she slid off her mount. A groom hurried forward to greet his master, bowing in customary deference, while at the same time he smiled broadly, showing his pleasure in his master's return. Richard gave the man a friendly nod and threw the reins to him, then turning to Alicia he offered her his arm.

'Allow me to escort you into your new home.'

She was surprised to find that the house, though in the centre of London, had a large garden, surrounded by a high wall where several mature trees stood. It had an air of privacy. There were raised beds in which grew herbs, vegetables and flowers, the first of the roses were beginning to show colour, wafting their delicate scent into the warm air.

The house stood at the end of the garden, abutting the street and though not as large as Leet Castle, it was no mean dwelling. It was three storeys high, with a dozen windows set symmetrically in its brick walls. As they neared the attractively arched doorway, Alicia noticed two retainers were waiting there to greet their lord.

Sir Richard wasted little time in introducing these more important servants of the household to Alicia. If they were astonished to realise her sex, clad as she was in tunic, hose and cloak, they were too well trained to show it. They made their obeisances with due humility, yet in a relaxed and smiling way that suggested a loyalty and affection for their master that she found pleasing. The servants followed as Richard escorted Alicia into the house.

'Bring refreshments for my lady,' Sir Richard ordered. 'And see that the victuals for the evening meal are good.'

He turned to her and as he did so ushered forward a man of middle age, who hurried into the great hall to meet them.

'This is William, my steward.'

William bowed gravely and Alicia acknowledged him with a gracious inclination of the head.

'We had not expected your arrival so soon, my lord,' William said. 'But the household is always ready to receive you, as you know.'

'Thank you, William. It's always a pleasure to return to such a well-ordered house. Have the best bed-chamber prepared for Lady Alicia.'

'That I will see to immediately.'

William departed and Richard conducted Alicia to a chair.

'Please—be at ease, Lady Alicia. I regret it's necessary for me to depart almost immediately on a matter of urgent business, but you'll be well looked after here.'

'Thank you, Sir Richard. I'm sure I shall be very comfortable and contented.'

He nodded his head. A slight smile seemed to play on one corner of his lips, and he stood looking down at her in silence but with an expression of wry humour for a minute or more. She raised her eyebrows quizzically.

'My lady, I am mindful that there is a matter of business that still remains to be conducted between you and me.'

What could he be talking about? Anxiously she scanned his features.

'What is that, my lord?'

It was his turn to look a little incredulous.

'You cannot have forgotten, surely, Alicia? It's the question you yourself brought up the night before last. The matter of our marriage.'

Her heart leapt. Had she really mentioned such a subject to him? Surely she had not been so forward? Her eyes wide and searching, she stared at him, wondering, trying to recall—and that look of wicked mockery that she read on his autocratic face put her into a state of confusion. Suddenly her own words came back to her with startling vividness—*I will not be bedded before I am wedded*.

Hot colour suffused her face and she found herself unable to meet his eyes. He gave a soft laugh, a laugh that was sensual and provocative, and the desire that was in his eyes kindled a hope in her breast. Was it possible that he felt the same about her as she did about him? But no word of love substantiated that look.

'I see you have not forgotten,' he said.

'I—I had not expected—' she murmured, then broke off.

She scanned his face, scarcely able to believe that he meant what he said. He had not till then made any mention of marriage—what could have happened to bring him to this decision?

'What had you not expected?' he asked coolly.

Honesty forced the admission from her. 'I had not expected you would wish to wed me when I have no dowry.'

'I have no time to talk of that now. I merely wish to inform you that I shall make the necessary arrangements immediately.'

The humour left his face. Those words seemed to sever any emotional tie that might have been struggling to life. Of course, she was well aware that marriages were purely business contracts, but she wished he had not spoken of it quite so matter-of-factly. He was as remote from her as he had ever been. His mouth settled into hard, cruel lines as he continued.

'I have no doubt that by now Leet will be in the hands of Rufus Blount and Sir Kimball—curse them both. It infuriates me to think of those swine

occupying what is rightfully my place. I must seek
audience with the king straight away. My good
friend Brian will have negotiated the surrender and
I trust he will have managed to obtain a safe
withdrawal for himself—'

'Yes, indeed, sire. You must go at once. I understand that and I shall pray that you will get all the
assistance that you require.'

'I may not return this night, for there is much to
be done. I'll bring you some more becoming
apparel and William will send you a girl to be your
maid. We shall seek the services of a priest before
whom we can plight our troth—we shall be wedded
on the morrow. Sleep well, Alicia.'

With that, he swung round and strode from the
house. Alicia stared in dismay at his departing
figure, feeling bewildered and helpless. She should
have been overjoyed at the prospect of being married to this man, for certainly she loved him with a
depth of feeling that she would never have believed
possible. She wished for no other fate—and yet, it
all seemed so precipitate, so quick, almost careless.

She knew so little about him. Even last evening
there had been mention once again of that woman
and it had seemed clear, so disturbingly clear, that
Elizabeth, whoever she was, meant a great deal to
Richard. Yet now, suddenly, he had asked her to
marry him—nay, not even asked. Simply made
arrangements for her to marry him. He knew full
well that her uncle would never part with anything
for a dowry under these circumstances—so why? If
only she could believe that he loved her she would
be the happiest girl in the land—but how could she
believe that, when his thoughts were so often
centred, not on her, but on—Elizabeth.

Presently a servant brought her a glass and a bottle of wine and a dish on which were several delectable little cakes. She took one small glass of wine and ate one of the cakes. She gazed around, still scarcely able to believe that soon, as Richard's wife, she would be mistress of this lovely house.

The great hall was on the ground floor, with windows that looked into the gardens. Its walls were hung with tapestries as rich as those in Leet, and their presence gave Alicia an indication that Sir Richard was by no means a poor man—but for how long would he remain so? The capture of Leet by Sir Hobart and Rufus Blount, if it were permanent, would undoubtedly mean a great financial loss, for much of the money that went to maintain this town house must come from the farms and lands around Leet.

Great fireplaces were set in the end walls. The beams of the ceiling had been chamfered in a rounded design that was very pleasant and in addition to the heavy trestle tables, which the servants were already setting up, there were two armchairs, a cupboard carved with birds and foliage and a large oak chest. It was rather more furniture than Alicia was accustomed to seeing in the sparsely filled rooms of country houses.

The girl who was sent to attend Alicia as her personal maid was young, no more than fifteen, and her name was Ellen. She was the daughter of a yeoman and had been sent to the Calder household to be 'trained in her manners', just as Alicia herself had been when she was younger.

'Mistress,' the child gave a deep curtsy.

Alicia indicated with a gentle movement of her hand that the girl should stand up and it seemed completely natural that they should smile at each other. Ellen could never take Jenny's place, but there was something very likeable about her.

'Perhaps my lady would like to wash and prepare to change after her journey,' suggested Ellen.

'Indeed I should,' Alicia agreed readily.

'Then I shall conduct you to your bed-chamber and fetch hot water for you,' said Ellen.

Alicia followed her willingly. She felt dusty after the journey, the leather of the reins had stained her hands, and she was glad to reach the privacy of the elegant room to which Ellen led her. With the maid's assistance she stripped off those masculine garments.

'You must be wondering why I travelled in this strange garb,' Alicia said. 'It was necessary because Leet Castle was being attacked and we had to flee under cover of darkness and escape through the enemy lines.'

'Oh, my lady—you must have been terrified! I know I should have been,' said Ellen, wide-eyed just to imagine it.

'Yes. I was very much afraid,' Alicia admitted.

Ellen chatted on as she prepared a bowl of warm water perfumed with rosemary for Alicia to wash. It was restful and pleasant.

'You must be tired, my lady,' exclaimed Ellen, with ready sympathy. 'It's such a long journey from Leet.'

Alicia nodded. 'Indeed I am, Ellen. We've ridden hard these past two days. I really feel so weary I've no wish to go down to the great hall for supper.'

'Shall I bring you something to eat on a tray, my lady?'

'Yes, please.'

She was too weary to eat much and when Ellen came into the room later in the evening, Alicia was already sleeping soundly.

When she awoke the next morning the sun was streaming in through the diamond panes of the window. Suddenly she sat bolt upright as she remembered that today Richard had said they were to be married. It seemed so unreal that she almost believed she must have dreamt it. She blinked her eyes, but there was no mistaking the reality of this room, it was the most imposing she had ever been in. Last night it had been too dark and she too tired for her really to appreciate it. Its walls were hung with Arras tapestries, and the bed had four solid carved posts which held up a magnificent canopy on which was a tapestry with a pastoral scene of nymphs and shepherds disporting themselves in a beautiful woodland setting.

She had slept naked and as she got up she took a coverlet from the bed, wrapped it round herself, and walked over to the window. The street below was thronging with people, horses, carts and urchins who darted here and there, and she could hear the shouts of pedlars calling their wares.

There came a knock on the door and Ellen entered. Her arms were filled with garments, and with expressions of delight she began to spread them over the bed for Alicia's inspection.

'Good morning, my lady. My lord asked me to bring these to you. Aren't they beautiful? Such fine material—such elegance!'

Alicia gazed at the clothes and felt only a stunned disbelief. She recognised that gown immediately. It was of deep red, with an elaborate design in gold thread—it was the same one that woman had worn on the evening Alicia arrived at Leet. She had not the slightest doubt in her mind. These clothes belonged—just as those she had previously worn—to Elizabeth. She eyed them with repugnance.

'My lady! Do you not like them?' asked Ellen, looking bewildered that Alicia did not share her delight in the garments. 'They are of the very latest fashion, I assure you—and they will be most becoming.'

Alicia gave a deep sigh. For a moment she could not bring herself to speak, even to answer Ellen's ingenuous question. She turned her back on the room and stood staring out of the window, but this time she saw nothing, her eyes were blinded by tears. All she could think was—he has been to see her!

She felt angry and humiliated. Should she confront him with what she knew? Did he think she was stupid that she would not know, would not question, whose clothes these were? She remembered how eagerly he had listened when Cedric Clifton had told him that Elizabeth was in London. How fast they had ridden yesterday—he had spared neither her nor their horses in his haste to get here. He had left almost immediately, pausing only to tell her that he would arrange their marriage while he was away. How empty that prospect seemed.

Yet, what could she do? She had forfeited her right to any dowry her uncle might have given her. Without one no one would be likely to marry her and, as she had said before, the only other prospect would be to go into a nunnery.

At that thought she was forced to shake her head. With her natural rebelliousness, how would she manage to cope with the repression of all self-will that the life of a nun demanded? She who could not even resist escaping to walk in the woods on a fine day—how could she imagine that she could fit herself to life in a convent? Perhaps at some later date—but not now. There was no way other than that which Sir Richard had offered her—and for that she should be grateful.

She just wished she could understand why he had offered to marry her. The only possible explanation she could think of was that he was sorry for her. Yes, that must be the reason. Her plight had aroused his pity. He had been forced to accept responsibility for her when she arrived at Leet. She had thrown herself on his mercy completely by that precipitate action and now, as a gallant knight, he had chosen marriage as the only way to protect her.

What a hopeless situation she had landed herself in! If only she had not grown to love him—impossible to check the thought. She had to admit it, a spark had been ignited somewhere in the very core of her being that day they had met in the woods. Since then it had been fanned into a flame of passion, every day spent in his company fettering her to him with silken threads of love. How could something so fragile hold with such strength, cut with such an excruciating bite, bring so much misery?

With an enormous effort of will-power she checked the tears, and wiped them away with a pretence of blowing her nose. Then she squared her shoulders and, forcing a smile, turned to face Ellen once again. Probably the little maid was aware that Alicia was distressed, but except for one quick searching look she dropped her eyes and made no comment.

'I am ready, Ellen. You may help me to get dressed.'

Half an hour later she descended to the great hall. There was no sign of Richard. Alicia stood, looking around her uncertainly, and William the steward hurried over to her.

'Good-morrow, my lady. I trust you slept well?'

'Very well, thank you, William. Where is my lord?'

'Sir Richard had to go out on a matter of business, my lady. He bade me to see to any requirements you might have, and said he would return as soon as possible. Will you take breakfast?'

'No, thank you, William.'

'Shall we sit in the solar to await my lord's return,' suggested Ellen.

'Very well,' agreed Alicia.

Ellen chattered but Alicia scarcely heard her. Slowly the morning wore away. At noon a servant brought them a tray with food and drink. Alicia forced herself to eat a little but she had no stomach for much. Her thoughts and emotions were so jumbled, and waiting was very tedious. It was mid-afternoon before word came that Sir Richard waited for her below. Again she descended the stair. He stood with his legs slightly apart, strong and muscular in dark blue hose, his large lithe body held taut—he always looked as if he was about to spring into violent action. She noticed how tall he was, head held high, autocratic, very much the lord of the household—her lord. She trembled at the thought.

'Come, Alicia,' he said as if he was in a hurry to get on with the matter. 'I have sent a message to the priest. He is even now waiting for us.'

He placed his hand on her elbow and guided her

out of the door into the street. She lifted her skirts to keep them clear of the rubbish that was strewn there, the odours of which were far from pleasant. Fortunately it was but a short walk to the church, and there the priest met them at the door. His black cassock was rusty with age and neglect, in hands that were neither steady nor clean he held a battered prayer-book. He peered at them with watery eyes.

'Are you the couple that's to be joined in wed-lock?' he asked.

'We are,' said Richard briefly. 'Pray proceed without delay.'

'It'll cost you more as you haven't had the banns read,' the priest pointed out.

'That is agreed,' Richard replied readily.

A clerk came out of the church and took his place beside the priest as he began the brief ceremony. He mumbled words which at first Alicia could scarcely understand, and so fast that it seemed he was anxious to get the business over as quickly as possible. Fortunately he slowed his voice when it came to the actual making of the vows.

'Richard Calder—hast thou will to have this woman to thy wedded wife?'

'Yes, sir.'

'And do you know of any reason why you may not come together with this woman, Alicia Bartolf?'

'No, sir.'

He repeated similar questions to Alicia, and she answered in the same way. Then he spoke again to Richard.

'Then will you best love her and hold ye to her and to no other to thy life's end?'

'Yes,' replied Richard firmly.

Did he really mean that, Alicia wondered? How many men kept that vow, though they made it in all earnestness?

'Now take the lady's hand and repeat after me—I Richard Calder, take thee Alicia Bartolf—'

He paused, and Alicia glanced at Richard's handsome profile and his face seemed expressionless as he repeated the vows. The feeling of unreality she had experienced when she awoke that morning returned. It was almost as if she was outside her own body, listening to the toneless, even, repetition with which Richard pledged himself.

'—in form of holy church to my wedded wife forsaking all other, holding me wholly to thee, in sickness and in health, in riches and in poverty, in well and in woe, till death us do part, and thereto I plight ye my troth.'

Then Alicia in turn made her vows. With a soft voice she repeated the words and knew that for her they were completely binding and final. Not only did love tie her to this man at her side, from now on the law upheld that. She became his possession utterly.

'Have you a ring? It is not necessary, but—'

'I have a ring.'

It was a gold band studded with tiny sapphires. Richard began to push it on to the third finger of her left hand, and that touch brought her back to reality. It was a proof that this simple ceremony had truly happened. The ring was a little too large but very pretty.

The priest led them into the church. Alicia knelt to pray while he entered the details of their wedding and eagerly took his fee. Man and wife, Richard and Alicia returned to his house.

CHAPTER
EIGHT

Such a brief ceremony, conducted as was usual at the church door, yet it complied with all that was required to make a marriage legal and binding. They had plighted their troth before two witnesses—now no one could put them asunder. It had all been so matter-of-fact that Alicia felt like pinching herself to make sure she really was awake, as with her hand lightly placed on Richard's arm she walked with him back to the house.

A part of her wanted to rejoice, told her this should be the happiest day of her life, but her actual feelings were numbed. She felt unable to comprehend, certainly unable to make sense of, this marriage. All the time she kept thinking how little joy had been expressed in the union and above all she wished that there had been some mention of love when it had been arranged. They approached the house and Sir Richard made a sweeping bow.

'Pray enter, my lady—my lady Calder.'

He smiled at her. It was the only trace of intimacy that had occurred between them during this, their wedding day. He ushered her immediately into the great hall. To the astonished retainers who were putting the finishing touches to the repast, he announced in ringing tones.

'This is my lady—Lady Alicia Calder—my wife.'

Spontaneously a cheer rose from all who were there, and the sound brought other servants running from the kitchens to see what the excitement was all about. The news was quickly told.

'Fill your tankards, all of you, and drink a toast to my lady and me,' called Sir Richard.

They certainly needed no encouragement, and no time was wasted in fetching the frothing liquid from the cellars in great pitchers and pouring it into drinking vessels.

Then the voice of William the steward rang out—'To my lord and lady—may they have long life, good health, prosperity and a fruitful union.'

Shyly Alicia lowered her eyes.

'To my lord and lady.'

Readily the toast was echoed and the ale quaffed down.

'Come—let us eat.'

Without more ado Sir Richard led Alicia to the top of the long table and seated her on his right hand. William took his place next to her and then all the other servants sat down on long benches, except for those who were serving. Soon the food was carried in and placed on the table. The linen cloth was of finest quality, and the knives and spoons of silver—at least for those at the top of the table, lower down they were made of bone. In the same way, Alicia and Richard and a few of the more important members of the household ate from silver platters, while those lower down used wooden ones.

Alicia scarcely knew what she ate that evening. Her usual healthy appetite deserted her, for the events had been quite bewildering, not only in themselves, but also in the speed with which they had happened. Particularly it played on her mind that she was clad in garments that rightfully belonged to that other lady, Elizabeth.

Elizabeth who? There was no answer to the question that plagued her mind. Neither was there any explanation she could think of for Richard's rush to visit that woman, except for the obvious one that he was deeply in love with her. Alicia found it equally inexplicable that he had married her, with no dowry. No doubt it was honourable of Richard to take her to wife, an act of great chivalry—though it made her even more sure that the lady he really loved must be unattainable.

Perhaps that was something for which she should be grateful. She sighed. She simply could make no sense of it. Of course, she knew that marriage had little to do with love—yet she admitted in her heart that she had always hoped that her husband would love her. Perhaps, in time, he would come to feel a true and deep affection for her if she were an obedient and willing wife. Of one thing at least she could be glad—she could, nay did, love this man who was now her husband. She resolved to do her utmost to please him, and remembered with a small flutter of her heart that soon she would be lying in his arms.

As the meal ended, the minstrels came forward to play to them and the jester began to caper and joke. He was quite a funny little man in his costume that was half yellow and half red with his hat with bells that jangled from each of its three peaks as they did also from the turned-up toes of his shoes. Alicia smiled at his antics. Sir Richard leaned towards her.

'Do you find them amusing?'

'Oh yes—and the minstrel has a pleasant touch too.'

'For my part I would rather be alone—with my wife.'

His voice came softly and sweetly to her ears. His face was only a few inches from her own and he regarded her with an expression in which the languid droop of his eyelids only half hid the twinkle of excitement. Her heart leapt in quick response. It was a look that awoke a racing emotion that made her feel totally feminine, and it seemed to probe deep into her soul. She had no doubt that he could read the love that shone in her face—there was no way she could hide that. He smiled with satisfaction. Demurely she lowered her eyes, but she knew what was required of her.

She stood up and prepared to withdraw. At once Ellen followed, two paces behind, up to that great bed-chamber. A fire burned in the hearth, even though it was not really a cold night, and the bed looked even more grand and imposing than she remembered. There was something intensely sensual about that bed. The sight of it, the implication of it, made her knees feel weak. She sat down on a stool.

'Shall I undress you, my lady?' inquired Ellen.

Alicia nodded. The little maid began at once to unravel the long lengths of fine muslin that draped over the butterfly headdress and to remove the frame that held it in position. She unpinned Alicia's hair and, catching it as it fell around her mistress's shoulders, Ellen parted it in two thick bunches and placed them to fall forward so that she could set to unfastening the strings with which her gown was laced up at the back.

Alicia sat patiently. Ellen seemed to be taking a

very long time over what should be a simple operation. She was sweet and attentive, but on this night of all nights Alicia missed the familiar touch and voice of Jenny. She hoped with all her heart that all was well with her and Reuben and said a silent prayer for their safety. Ellen gave a harder tug at the strings of the gown. Really the child was quite clumsy.

'What is happening, Ellen?' Alicia asked.

'Oh, my lady—it has gone into a knot.'

'Can you not untie it?'

'I—I can't. Oh dear—what ever shall I do?'

She began to cry.

'Shh!' soothed Alicia, though a panic began to rise in her own breast. 'Calm yourself. Try and ease it open.'

'I've been trying and trying—but it just seems to get itself tighter and tighter.'

Ellen sniffed and took out a kerchief to wipe her eyes, and then began again to try and unfasten the knot that held the gown so tightly to Alicia's figure, pulling it tighter than ever as she tugged at the strings. Still it would not loosen.

The door of the chamber opened. Alicia swung round. There stood Sir Richard. He had removed his doublet and waistcoat and was clad only in his shirt and breeches. Behind him came a manservant carrying his clothes and his sword.

'What's this, then?' he demanded. 'Truly I thought you'd had time—'

Alicia rose and, as was natural, to emphasise her apology she lowered herself in a deep curtsy before him.

'My lord—'tis but an accident—with the gown. The strings have knotted—'

Sir Richard strode forward and inspected the recalcitrant fastenings. He beckoned the man-servant forward and took the sword from him, unsheathing it with a sure hand.

'Oh, my lord—you'll ruin the gown,' Ellen cried.

'No matter, so long as I don't ruin my lady's pretty back,' Sir Richard said. 'You can buy materials for all the new gowns you require tomorrow. Keep very still, Lady Alicia.'

She felt nothing, as without the least touch to her skin, the tip of the sword severed the strings of the gown down the whole length of her back. At once the gown fell open and Alicia clutched it to her in instinctive modesty.

Richard gave a light laugh, as though amused at her predicament. 'Relax—'tis done.'

He threw the sword hilt first towards the man-servant, who caught it with a practised hand, re-placed it in its scabbard and then withdrew.

'You may also retire,' Sir Richard ordered Ellen.

'But my lord—I haven't yet finished attending to my lady—'

'Go.' His voice was imperative.

The little maid bobbed a hasty curtsy.

'Yes, my lord. Thank you, my lord.'

She hurried out of the room, grateful that her clumsiness had not resulted in some punishment. The door was closed. Alicia stood very still, her eyes downcast.

Richard came to stand close before her and with a hand that was gentle, he lifted her face, so that she had to look at him. Then he bent his head and his lips claimed hers in a kiss. Softly his mouth touched hers and she tasted its sweetness with wonderment, as if she was in a dream. Gently he took her into his arms and she experienced a joy beyond the normal tenor of life.

Then, as passion flared in him, she felt his body tense and his arms closed more firmly around her, crushing her close. His lips began to press with a stronger and firmer force until she had to open her mouth. Still he held her, still his mouth clung to hers in that ecstatic kiss as if he would never let her go.

Instinctively she responded to him, moved her body sinuously to the caressing movements of his hands, which had slipped beneath the slashed back fastenings of her gown, stroking the silky shift which was so fine that he might almost have been touching her bare skin. He was experienced in love-making. She recognised that, even in her innocence. She felt no jealousy at that moment, for her world was all delight, deep and unfathomable, as if she swam in a brilliant sea of sensuality.

At last he lifted his head. Breathless she gazed at him and studied him feature by feature and loved everything that went to make up his handsome face. Those eyes, so dark brown, yet, she now noticed, had tiny flecks of gold in them—and his eyebrows quirked fascinatingly above, fringing the strong bone of his forehead. His nose, straight and uncompromising—surely the most handsome nose she had ever seen. She lifted one exploratory finger, like a child, to run it over the shapely pink sensitiveness of his lips and, as she did so, his mouth lifted slightly at the corners in a smile that was sweetly tender.

He loosed his arms from about her, yet still held her close to him, needing only the compelling power of his eyes, the magnetism of his masculinity—it would have been no more possible for her to move away from him than if she had been held in chains of iron. She stood, meekly submissive, as he pushed down the bodice of her gown. Her whole desire was to give him pleasure, and willingly in response to his unspoken wish she pulled her arms from the close-fitting sleeves. The gown fell at her feet and she was clad only in the silken shift.

'Sweet Alicia,' he murmured.

She could feel the excitement in his fingers—they trembled just a little as he pulled at the string which was the only fastening of that diaphanous under-garment. It was tied in a simple bow at the neck and opened easily. In a moment that too was lying at her feet.

Then Richard was showering her with kisses, kissing her face and her neck—down to her breasts, and the touch of his lips there was so exquisite that it brought a low moan from her throat.

He swept her up in his arms and lifted her off her feet, and her arms curled themselves naturally around his neck, her whole being was centred on him. She could feel the warmth of his skin through the fine linen of his shirt, smell the musky maleness of his body as he held her close.

He took her over to the great four-poster. The covers had already been turned back and he placed her in the softness of the feather-bed. Then he straightened himself and stood looking down at her, and the pleasure she read in his eyes was a joy for her to behold. He did not find her thin and plain—all she saw in his face told her that to him she was beautiful—desirable—beddable.

A knock came at the door. Sir Richard swung round and swore.

'Who the devil dares—?'

He broke off as the knock came again, louder, more insistently. The voice of William the steward came through the heavy wooden panels of the door.

'My lord—I beg your pardon—'

Richard strode across the room and flung it open. Alicia clutched the bedclothes over herself and kept low in the softly enveloping feather-bed.

'What is it?' The note of impatience was edged with anger in Richard's voice.

'A message, sire—'

William's voice was lowered and Alicia could not hear his next words. 'What is it? Surely it can wait—'

'I fear not, sire. I would not have presumed to disturb you if it had not been imperative that you go without delay.'

'At this time of night?'

'Sire—it is not really so late. The messenger came from my lady Elizabeth and she entreats you to respond immediately.'

No more persuasion was needed.

'Send my man to help me to dress,' commanded Richard.

'Shall I accompany you, sire?'

'No. It's best that I go alone. Now wait outside.'

Alicia lay, deep and troubled, in the great bed, her hair spread over the pillow and the sheets held tight just below her small defiant chin. All the intimacy that had been between them, so warm and natural, had frozen and fractured. Elizabeth! The very name stirred a fury of anger in Alicia's heart that was quite out of character for her.

'You heard that message—I regret that I have to leave you, temporarily.'

He returned to the bedside as he spoke. Again he stood looking down at her, but now only her face with its great wide, wondering eyes was visible above the tightly held coverlet. He seemed scarcely to notice. His thoughts were already elsewhere. She fought back the tears that welled up in her eyes—she did not wish him to see how much she cared. She swallowed hard and tried to make her voice sound normal.

'What is it, my lord? What does it all mean?'

'Nothing you need to concern yourself about.'

'I—I should like to know,' she pleaded.

'I have no time to explain. It is essential that I answer this summons straight away.' She stared up at him without moving.

Again a knock came on the door. It was his man-servant, come to help his master to dress, and Alicia noted that despite the need for urgency some care was taken that he was accoutred in his finest garments, his sword at his side. Evidently he intended to impress. Without another word he strode from the room.

She was left feeling bereft. He was the centre of her universe, she wanted nothing but to be with him and now she felt chilled and rejected. A cold dismay made her literally shiver, caused by the knowledge that—that woman, that Elizabeth, was again involved. As soon as her name was mentioned Richard had been all eagerness to respond to the summons.

The hatred—yes, she had to admit to herself, it was hatred, wicked though it was to harbour such thoughts, the hatred that Alicia felt for Elizabeth

began to grow and almost at once those vitriolic
thoughts spilled over to Richard as well. How dare
he use her thus! He had no care for her, that was
quite obvious, or he would not treat her so.

Those vows he had spoken only a few hours ago
had been meaningless, except inasmuch as the law
still bound them together. That passion which had
been swathed so comfortingly around her was revealed as a mere illusion. There had been no real
love in it. It had been an animal desire which no
doubt would rise again, like a hunger or thirst, that
her body would assuage, but which would leave her
soul bleeding. The future loomed miserably before
her. She turned over and buried her face in the
pillow as tears welled up and spilled over in a
torrent of weeping.

Eventually she must have fallen asleep. When
she awoke she was still alone in the great bed and
Ellen was busying herself, seated by the window
with Elizabeth's gown on her knee, her needle
plying swiftly. She looked up and saw that her
mistress was awake.

'My lady. I don't know what to do with this.' She
stood up and held out the gown, showing where Sir
Richard's sword had slashed some of the eyelets
through which the laces should be threaded to
fasten it.

'I've been trying and trying to mend it, but
whatever I do I fear it will show.'

The last thing Alicia wanted to be bothered
about at that particular time was her gown.

'No matter,' she said. 'I'm sure it will do well
enough.'

'It really is not fitting, for my lady's position—
suppose you were to be invited out to one of the

great houses? We must see at once about some new garments for you.'

'Must we?' Alicia said.

'Don't you remember that last evening my lord gave me instructions that we were to buy all that we needed to make a completely new wardrobe for you?'

Listlessly Alicia looked at Ellen, and the little maid's face was so full of eager anticipation at the prospect of the shopping expedition that she could not help smiling a little. Ellen took that as a good sign, and full of self-importance and an ingenuous pride at her own competence pressed on to explain the arrangements she had already made.

'I have spoken to the steward, my lady—and told him of your needs. Some materials there are in the house already and I have instructed four girls to begin making shifts and stockings for you this morning. But for your outer garments I suggest that we go to the cloth mercer and see what materials he has to offer. Now I'll go and fetch you something to eat and drink, my lady.'

She did not wait for any response from Alicia, but having decided what was to be done that day, set about performing her duties, as though all was quite normal. Did Ellen know that Sir Richard had been called away so abruptly, Alicia wondered? Whether she did or not made no difference. If it had been Jenny she could have spoken of it, voiced her dismay, but with Ellen it was not quite the same and Alicia was aware that the girl had probably been in Sir Richard's household for several years— her loyalty would all be to him.

When the tray of food was brought, Alicia found enough appetite to eat a little and as she did so her spirits began to lift to something that more nearly approximated her normal self. She glanced down at her hands and started in dismay and alarm.

'My ring! It's gone. I kept it on when I went to bed last night—'

'I'll look, mistress.' Ellen turned back the bed-covers. 'Here it is. It must have slipped off your finger—'

'It's too big. I'm afraid I'll lose it. I'll wear it on the chain round my neck. Perhaps I can have it made smaller later on.'

She wondered what Richard would think if he noticed she was not wearing the ring on her finger—then shrugged. What did it matter? He had not returned, even yet. Whatever her feelings, brooding would do nothing to help, that was quite certain. She had no tears left.

She could even contemplate, dry-eyed, the fact that it was quite possible her husband had spent the night in Elizabeth's bed. The anguish induced by such a thought was too intense to be washed away by tears, but as she determined to face the facts that seemed to be staring at her, she began to feel angry, as well as hurt. The one emotion helped to assuage the other and gradually her mood changed to one of angry defiance.

'Right, Ellen,' she said, thrusting aside the tray and jumping to her feet. 'Let's set out at once and find this cloth mercer and see what he can offer.'

Ellen had obtained a letter from the steward instructing the merchant to supply all her needs—and that being so, Alicia had no intention of stinting herself. The maid had made a passably good job of repairing the one gown she then possessed and,

clad in it, with a shawl thrown over her shoulders to
hide the damage, she and Ellen walked the half
mile or so through the streets of London.

The merchant was delighted to have a customer
who was not only rich and in need of many clothes
but who was also quite willing to take his advice.
Alicia had previously had most of her garments
made from home-woven woollens and linens, except for her very best gown for which the material
had been bought in Norwich, where were some of
the finest weavers in the land. Now she was enchanted by the bright colours and rich embroidery
that was offered by the merchant. She hesitated to
choose between two types of material, both of
which seemed to her delightfully soft and silky, as
well as being woven in a bold and beautiful design.

'My lady, may I recommend the sarsenet,'
advised the merchant, holding up the unrolled end
of a bolt of beautiful crimson silk. 'It is very fine and
of such excellent quality that it will last a life-time,
whereas this harletry, though it be only forty pence
a yard, will not endure for two seasons.'

He emphasised his point by crumpling a corner
of the inferior, though quite attractive-looking,
stuff. Alicia smiled at him.

'I will have one of each,' she declared. 'Also I
shall need a cloak—or perhaps two, and something
for the mornings—'

Never before had she been able to order clothes
with such extravagance. Always when she had been
grudgingly fitted with a new gown by Aunt Margaret, the emphasis had been on thrift. Now in a
mood of wild carelessness, encouraged by Ellen,
who hoped her mistress when she tired of some of
the clothes might hand them down to her, she

ordered with gay abandon. She even began to take
an interest as, together with the obsequiously helpful merchant, they discussed the latest styles in
which gowns were being worn. It was also necessary to purchase headgear, and Alicia discovered
that the butterfly headdress she had been accustomed to wearing had gone out of favour with the
ladies of London. The steeple headdress was now
much more commonly worn, and in addition this
had lappets of contrasting material which framed
the face and hung down to the shoulders. She also
bought three girdles, one wide and embroidered,
another narrower and bejewelled and the third of
tawny silk with buckle and pendant.

When at last they left the cloth mercer it was
mid-afternoon and the street was thronging with
people. It was narrow and the houses seemed to
close in on them as they walked along. Alicia felt a
little nervous in such a crowd of strangers. She
lifted her skirts to prevent them from being soiled
on the filth that littered the cobbles. Little attempt
had been made to clear away the rubbish that
everyone tossed out of their houses and the smells
were quite distressing, especially to one who was
more accustomed to the fresh air of the country.
Ellen seemed scarcely to notice them at all. She
chatted on as excitedly as if the gowns that were
about to be made were for her instead of for her
mistress.

They were almost half-way back to Sir Richard's
house when a boy darted up to them. A ragged
urchin, barefoot and dirty, he caught hold of
Alicia's hand.

'My lady—come with me,' he said.

'Go away, you scoundrel.' Ellen gave him a

shove. 'I know your type. Be off with you and don't trouble decent folk.'

The boy ignored her and continued to tug at Alicia's arm.

'My lady—you are needed. My lord has been injured—'

His voice was breathless and urgent. Alicia stopped at once and stared at the boy. Her heart seemed to miss a beat.

'My lord who?' asked Ellen, sharply.

'My lord Calder,' the boy answered promptly.

'Where?' cried Alicia, her heart thumping like a wild bird within her rib-cage.

'I'll take you to him—this way.'

He tugged again at her hand, dragging her towards a narrow opening between high overhanging buildings. It gaped darkly, but Alicia began to follow.

'No, my lady,' Ellen pleaded. 'I don't trust him.'

She held on to Alicia's other arm, preventing her from moving.

'Don't be absurd, Ellen,' said Alicia, fear making her voice snap. 'I have to go to Sir Richard.'

She shook the restraining hand from her.

'Show me where my lord is,' she said to the boy.

'My lady—do have a care—' Ellen called and, as Alicia heeded her not, she began to follow her mistress.

Had Alicia not been rendered almost distraught by the news that Richard had been injured she might have listened to her maid's warning and held back. As it was she followed the urchin closely as he led her into the narrow, dark alley away from the busy main street. She was running now to keep up with the boy who, having persuaded Alicia to fol-

low, darted as swiftly as a stoat. The alley was high
walled, no shaft of sunlight penetrated it and the air
held within it seemed stagnant and fetid. Alicia
held her kerchief to her nose, but hurried on. Ellen
followed, well behind now, and glanced about fearfully, trying to persuade Alicia to stop.

'Wait, my lady—'

'Where is my lord?' cried Alicia to the boy.

'Just round the corner,' he urged.

'What has happened to him?'

The boy made no answer. He sped away round a
right-angled corner of the alley and Alicia followed. The passage opened out to a back street.
Ahead of them stood a carrier's cart, covered with a
hooped canvas top. A couple of men had been
lounging beside one of its heavy iron-shod wheels,
and she saw them straighten up as she ran towards
them. Then she felt a stab of fear, and this time it
was not for Richard, but because she sensed her
own danger. One of the men had looked directly at
her and she recognised him as a servant of her
uncle, Rufus Blount. In the same instant that she
knew him and was about to cry out in alarm, his
hands shot out and caught her. One powerful arm
pinioned her arms to her sides while the other hand
clamped over her mouth.

She could not cry out or beat her hands against
him, but she could kick and she did so with a vigour
that surprised and angered him. His grip tightened
till it seemed that all the breath would be squeezed
from her constricted chest.

'You vixen! Be still or it'll go ill with you.'

Wild-eyed she stared into his ugly face and saw
that he meant what he said. The second man took
hold of her ankles and unceremoniously she was

bundled into the back of the carrier's cart. Both men clambered in beside her, holding her so effectively that she had no chance of escape or to shout for help—though there seemed to be no one about in that back street—no one who could have gone to her aid, even if she had been able to scream. Ellen had been right. She had been led straight into a trap.

'Where's the other bitch?' snarled the first man.

'Got away. Ran back down that alley. Barney's gone after her.'

They must be speaking of Ellen. She had evidently turned and run for it. Even at that moment, however, Alicia heard a shout from the driver and the cart jolted forward.

'This is the one my lord Blount wants. But I reckon Barney'll catch the servant girl—and he'll know how to deal with her to keep her from talking.'

As he spoke, the first man unwound a none too clean kerchief from his neck and began to wrap it over Alicia's mouth in a gag. She kicked again as violently as she could, but was at once dealt such a heavy blow across both her legs that she seemed almost paralysed.

'Lie still, I tell yer, if you don't want to get hurt bad,' the man growled. 'You may as well know our orders are to take you back alive—that's all. We weren't given any instructions as to how we did it.'

Alicia lay still. She was scared stiff and knew herself to be utterly helpless. Having effectively silenced her with that foul-smelling gag, the men proceeded systematically to tie her legs together at the ankles and to rope her crossed wrists. She lay on her back as the cart jolted over the rough streets, deep in potholes into which the wheels sank half to the axle. The wooden floor of the cart bumped and bruised her every yard of the way—they were taking her back to her uncle, Rufus Blount. She was absolutely terrified and there was no way of escape.

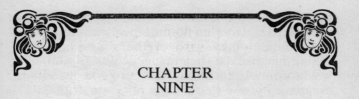

CHAPTER
NINE

THE CART rumbled on. It seemed as if it would
never stop. Alicia lost all concept of time, she was
in such pain. She could only lie and moan beneath
the gag. Every bone in her body seemed to be
jarred by the planks on which she lay and the ropes
were so tight they cut into her flesh.

What would happen to her now, she wondered?
She drew small comfort from the stark fact that her
uncle had requested she should be taken back to
him alive, though she believed those ruffians who
now held her would have had no scruples had their
orders been otherwise. They would have slain her
and disposed of her body without a qualm.

At last the cart came to a stop. There was the
sound of voices outside. Then the end canvas
covers of the cart were thrust apart and Alicia's
captors jumped out and dragged her out after
them. With no ceremony the man who seemed to
be the leader of the two slung her over his shoulder
so that her head hung down behind his back and,
holding her legs close to his chest, walked away
from the cart.

Alicia tried to lift her head and take a quick
glance around. They were in an enclosed courtyard, with stables and a high wall. A moment later
the man was ascending a short flight of steps and
entered the house. She could only hang there as

helpless as a sack of turnips as he proceeded along a short corridor and then entered a small chamber. There he bent down to heave her off his back and dumped her on the floor.

'My lord—I think these are the goods you bade me fetch. I regret that she did not come willingly.'

'I'll warrant that she didn't!'

That was the grating snarl of her uncle. She looked up, and the terror she felt must have shown in her eyes, for he gave a laugh that was as ugly as the face that bent over her. What was he doing here? The cart had not travelled far, so she must still be in London. She had assumed that Rufus Blount, after taking Leet, would have stayed there for some time.

'Well, wench—we have some unfinished business that concerns you, have we not?'

She couldn't answer him because of the gag that seemed to get tighter and more painful with every passing minute. She would have liked to spit in his eye, but of course there was no chance of doing that either. She made a small sound which she hoped might induce him to remove the filthy kerchief, but Rufus was in no hurry to do that. He turned to the ruffian who had carried her in.

'You've done well. Now go.' The man began to withdraw, but Rufus called after him. 'Tell Sir Hobart and the priest that we'll be ready for the ceremony in five minutes.'

What was he saying? What ceremony? Why did he need a priest? Were they going to kill her? Terror filled her heart. She heard the heavy footsteps of the man leaving the room. Then her uncle's angry, distorted face was bending over her again.

'You wretched creature. I'd like to beat you black and blue for what you've done, for the trouble you've put me to. You're nothing but an ungrateful shrew.'

He raised his fist as he spoke and for a moment Alicia thought he would not be able to contain his fury. She tried not to flinch, but it was impossible, and her fear seemed to give Rufus Blount some satisfaction.

'You may well look frightened, my girl. It takes all my self-control to keep my hands off you, but that is a pleasure I reckon I should leave to your husband.'

Her husband? Richard—was he here? She felt as if reason had deserted her. She tried to look round, turning her head as far as she could to one side and then the other. There appeared to be no one in the room with them.

Rufus knelt beside her and with rough fingers jerked and pulled at the knots that held the kerchief so tightly. He ripped the cloth away and a trickle of blood ran from one corner of her mouth where, in his uncaring clumsiness, he caused her lip to split. With her hands still tied, she could do nothing to wipe it away. She moved her mouth gingerly; it felt numb and bruised, ran her tongue around to moisten her dry lips.

Rufus Blount carried on with undoing the knots in the rope that bound her wrists and ankles. She watched him and waited. There was nothing that she had to say to this man who had been her oppressor for so long.

'Stand up, wench,' he commanded.

Silently she obeyed, rubbing her aching joints which had been bound so cruelly tight that they had stiffened, even in that short time. She stumbled as she got to her feet, but he made no move to support or assist her.

'Mayhap that's taken a little of the fight out of you, my fine lady,' he laughed.

She lifted her head and gazed at him steadfastly, with a touch of her old defiance returning. She was bruised and sore and terrified—but she was not yet beaten. She said nothing. The habit of silent acceptance that was considered the right attitude for children and women had been taught through years of brutal punishments. The smallest word or deed that might appear to be rebellious, questioning the authority of the dominant males or the older women, could result in a rain of blows, of beatings, that left weals open for days. She had suffered such assaults in the past and had learned that sometimes it was safest to remain silent. She knew she was helpless in her uncle's hands and could only pray that God would give her strength to stand whatever trials came to her.

She looked round, wondering where she was. It was a beautifully proportioned room with elaborately curving beams in the roof and some panelling at the far end where a wide window, bright with stained glass, let in the afternoon light. Something in the colour and pattern of the heraldic designs there seemed familiar. She stared at it for some minutes—the reds and blues were vivid—surely she had seen that design before, or was it simply one like it? She was not close enough to be sure. She judged that the house was fairly new and that it must belong to someone of wealth and consequence. Although her uncle had from time to time gone to London on business, Alicia had never accompanied him and she had not realised that he had such an elegant house. Her curiosity was aroused sufficiently for her to overcome her reticence.

'My lord, my uncle—where have you brought me?'

His lip curled derisively.

'Do you not remember it? This was the town house of your parents.'

Alicia's heart jumped. She had been right—it was her family coat of arms fashioned in stained glass in the window.

'And now it belongs to—?'

'As your guardian, it has been mine for the past few years, as has Braister Castle and the manors of Blakholm and Rusingham and Malletby. On your marriage, of course, they go to your husband—who now comes.'

Alicia swung round. Her eyes opened wide in horror and shock as the ungainly figure of Sir Hobart Kimball clumped heavily into the room, followed by a priest. The two men advanced towards Rufus and Alicia and the full import of their intentions became clear. They intended to force her to go through a marriage ceremony, just as they had planned before she had escaped from Braister.

'No!'

The single word burst from her lips and earned her a swipe from the hand of her uncle that made her stagger in its ferocity.

'Shut up, you slut. You should go down on your knees in gratitude that my lord Kimball is still willing to marry you, despite the way you've behaved.'

Sir Hobart was close enough now for her to see clearly all those features that she had found so repulsive before. He was dressed in a long gown that covered the whole of his paunchy figure and, though the weather was warm, it had decorations of fur at wrist and hem. He looked red and hot, his nose seemed even more bulbous than Alicia remembered it, and beside it was that scar that puckered his face to one side. Again, however, it was not only the ugliness of his face and figure that was so repulsive—it was the vicious expression in his eyes as he looked at her.

There was not one jot of affection or pleasure reflected there. His displeasure in her was matched by her own feelings towards him. Yet he was willing to go through this marriage ceremony—it was not she, but her lands and properties, that he was eager to acquire. Yet he was not without some pleasure in the anticipated match. There was a leer of sadistic satisfaction on his face. He was a bully and he was going to enjoy inflicting the maximum humiliation on her. His first words emphasised this.

'Ha! So you've got the baggage back, Rufus. A mettlesome filly takes some breaking—but 'tis a fight a man can take pleasure in. Let us waste no more time but get on with the ceremony. Come on, sir priest, where's your book of words?'

The priest was a tall thin man with a cadaverous face, and hands so bony they looked as if they belonged to a skeleton rather than to a living human. He was old and could move but slowly as he came forward.

'I am ready, sire. If you and the lady will just stand together—so—'

He attempted to move Alicia closer to Sir

Hobart, but she remained obstinately where she stood.

'I cannot marry this man,' she declared. 'I am already sworn to my lord, Richard Calder.'

For a moment there was a stunned silence.

'She lies,' shouted Rufus.

'No, my lord, my uncle. It was but yesterday at the church door, I plighted my troth—'

'At which church door?'

'I—I know not—'

'You see? I told you she lies.'

'Not so, my lord. It is true. Please send for my husband—'

'For that rogue? Never. He may think he's been clever, getting you to go through some form of ceremony to get hold of your lands, but he won't get away with it. You could not marry without my consent.'

Rufus Blount caught hold of her hand. He grasped it roughly, holding it up as if it was an object on display.

'If you're truly married as you say—where's your ring?'

Alicia pulled her hand away.

'I have a ring. Sir Richard put it on my finger during the ceremony, but it is too big. I have it on this cord at my neck.'

She pulled the ring up from where it had lain against her skin, beneath her bodice. She held it out for them to see.

'A likely tale! Any honestly married woman would wear her ring on her finger, for all the world to see.'

'I tell you it's too big. I was afraid I might lose it.'

Tears started into her eyes. Was there no way she could make them believe her? She turned to the priest.

'Please, sire, as you are a man of God—don't let them make me break the vows I have already made. I swear to you that I was married yesterday afternoon to Sir Richard Calder, at the door of a church, here in London.'

The priest shook his head.

'My dear, there are many, many, churches in London and I fear there are priests who will pretend to hear such vows, but they are meaningless, for I do not believe you would have the right to make them without the consent of your guardian. You know full well that your first duty in all matters is to obey your uncle.'

'Exactly,' said Rufus. 'You may have been tricked into some false declaration, but it can never be a true marriage.'

She gazed from one to the other in horror. It was not true, she was sure it was not true—she was legally married to Richard. The priest was joining with her uncle and Sir Hobart to trick her.

'I swear to you that I made my vows in all honesty, from my heart—'

'Enough of this nonsense, wench,' Sir Rufus snapped. 'You've heard the priest's words. By what right do you defy not only me, but the judgment of a man of the church?'

Alicia fell to her knees in supplication before the priest.

'Father, I swear to you that what I say is true. I have always understood that it is only necessary to make such a declaration before witnesses for it to be binding for life—aye and beyond it too, for all I know. So we did but yesterday, Sir Richard and I. Would you make me a bigamist?'

The priest looked troubled. He turned towards Rufus.

'If in truth the lady is already married, I could not perform the ceremony you wish.'

'Fool! Would you take the part of this sly wench against me?' screamed her uncle.

'Sire, if the lady has already exchanged vows with another, then she is no longer your ward, she belongs solely to her husband.'

Sir Hobart moved over to stand close to Alicia.

'I heard that Sir Richard was abroad last night, at the home of that whore, Elizabeth Woodville. Isn't that strange if you say he was wedded to you but a few hours earlier?'

Alicia gasped. What was he saying? Did all the world know that Richard was having an affair with Elizabeth Woodville? At last she knew the woman's full name. Before she could come to terms with all that those words implied she felt her arms gripped with hands so hard they bit into the flesh painfully.

'Well, you slut—what do you have to say to that?'

Dumbly she stared at her uncle. He began to shake her in his fury.

'Answer me, do you hear? Tell us truly—for all this wild talk of marriages, are you yet a virgin?'

'I—I—'

Her hesitation was more than enough for her uncle.

'There—what did I tell you?' he sneered. 'That was no marriage. Even if there was some cere-mony—which I doubt—it would be meaningless until it was consummated. You must see that in her wickedness of heart she's only seeking to persist in defying me. Let's have no more nonsense—get on with the wedding.'

'Sire—I could be unfrocked if I were found to have done such a thing.'

'There may be worse things to trouble you than being unfrocked.'

'My lords—I—I did not expect such complications when I agreed—'

The priest, whose face had seemed colourless before, actually blanched as Rufus interrupted him.

'We didn't pay your debts and get you released from the Fleet Prison for you to defy our wishes with your cant.'

'I—I will, my lord—but—'

The priest was obviously as terrified of Rufus as Alicia was—perhaps more so, for he was both elderly and frail. She guessed that it was because of these infirmities that he had been chosen. They had anticipated that Alicia would put up a resistance and therefore had found a man who was so close to breaking-point that they would be able to make him perform their evil will.

'No buts—get on with it.'

'I will, of course, perform the ceremony as you desire. I am a little hard of hearing and I cannot always be sure that my ears hear aright.'

'That's good enough—'

'But I only wish to say—it could be declared null and void if it is proved that the lady was in truth wedded yesterday.'

'No one will be able to prove that,' declared Rufus.

'How can you be so sure?' demanded Sir Hobart. 'If I am to enter into this alliance, then I must be absolutely certain that there will be no later disagreement.'

'Get on with the wedding. When you bed her this night you will know if she is a virgin or not. Why worry beyond that?'

' 'Tis tempting, Rufus—'

He moved a step closer to Alicia and she began to tremble in horror—she would sooner die than be touched by him. Then Sir Hobart halted, evidently having second thoughts, not quite trusting his friend, Rufus Blount.

'I am told Calder has recently acquired some powerful friends, and if he thinks he has a claim on all the Bartolf properties, he will not lightly give them up.'

Alicia drew in her breath sharply. Those words explained so much—what a fool she had been! Richard knew of her inheritance. He had probably become aware of it as soon as he knew her name, for he had made it his business to spy on Rufus Blount and probably knew quite a lot about his affairs. That had been the reason he had been so quick to take her to wife himself. It had not been pity for her that had inspired that decision—he had married her simply to acquire her lands and properties. She meant no more to him than she did to the hated Sir Hobart. Rufus was still exerting pressure because he needed the patronage of his friend's army to enable him to hold Leet and, very likely, to take other manors which he had his acquisitive eye on.

'I tell you, Hobart, you've no need to worry,' said Rufus. 'I know my niece. There has been no marriage in the proper sense of the word. Tell the truth, wench.'

He shook her again, determined to wrench a statement from her but Alicia stated the simple fact once more.

'I was married yesterday to Sir Richard Calder. We are joined and no man can put us asunder.'

It was the truth. It brought her no happiness, but it was the plain truth. For good or ill, just as her vows had declared, she was married to Richard.

'You lie. You lie! You'll suffer for this—you—you filthy slattern—'

He flung her from him with such force that she fell to the floor.

'Leave her to me, Hobart. I guarantee that within a day or two she'll be begging you to marry her and all this nonsense of a previous betrothal will have been forgotten.'

'That may be so.' Sir Hobart expressed no concern that his future wife should be submitted to such pressure; he was still concerned with the legal side of this marriage. 'Meanwhile I shall consult with my lawyer and discover whether in his opinion there has been a real marriage. If it isn't so, then I'll hold myself in readiness to perform my part of the bargain as soon as you send me word, Rufus.'

A shout from Rufus brought two men rushing in from where they must have been stationed, just outside the door.

'Take this wench and lock her in the strongroom,' he commanded. 'She is to have no meat or drink, but will stay there alone until she has learned better manners.'

Their hands were rough, and she winced as they picked her up, one grasping her shoulders and the

other supporting her feet, but she would not cry
out. She lay limp, making no struggle as they
carried her from the room. On they went through
the house, which was evidently quite extensive,
along a dark passage and finally down a stone
stairway where the chill sunless air smelled dank
and unwelcoming.

A heavy door was thrust open and Alicia
dumped inside on the cold stone floor. A moment
later the door was clanked shut and bolted on the
outside—she was alone in the dark. She shivered
and lay still, too terrified in that moment even to
stir an inch. She had no means of knowing where
she was, except that it was obviously underground.
Horrific thoughts of rats and beetles leapt into her
imagination and she drew her skirts close about
her.

Presently she became aware that there was a
chink of light coming through a small window set
high in one wall. It was unglazed and partly covered
with greenery that grew outside, so it was probably
at ground-level. As her eyes became accustomed to
the gloom, she realised she was imprisoned in a
bare cellar, without the least comfort, without even
the barest necessities of life. She shivered again.
Her uncle had said she was to be kept there until
she had learned to mend her ways—but how could
she? Even if she wished to agree to his monstrous
suggestion, it was a fact that she was married to
Richard.

Richard. Where was he now? Her world had
been shaken to its foundation. How could she have
come to love a man as hard and uncaring as he? Not
only did her uncle and Sir Hobart know of
Richard's liaison with Elizabeth—and now at last

she knew the woman's full name, Lady Elizabeth Woodville—but they had referred to her as a whore. Such epithets were commonplace when men lost their tempers, but in this case Alicia was inclined to believe it, for it confirmed her suspicions that Richard was involved in an amorous affair. Her uncle and Sir Hobart had even known that Richard had gone to Elizabeth last night. How could they have known that? They must have been keeping watch on his movements. Their plans had obviously been made with care and cunning, and but for her assertion that she was already married there was no doubt that, with or without her consent, some sort of wedding ceremony would have been performed and she would by now be completely at the mercy of the brutal Sir Hobart Kimball.

Her mental agony was deepened by that flash of enlightenment—Richard had married her merely in order to acquire her property. She had no doubt that that was the true reason for the speed with which he had hurried her to the priest. Perhaps he had feared that Rufus might try to get her back, and had therefore decided to wed her himself immediately. What a fool she had been to imagine that any man would marry her without a dowry. She moaned aloud at such unbearable thoughts, then got to her feet and began to pace over the hard stone floor.

She moved towards the window. It was too high in the wall for her to see out, and, besides being so narrow, it was heavily barred. Certainly it offered no chance of escape. She searched for something to stand on, but the room seemed to be quite empty except for a chest that was far too heavy for her even to drag nearer to the window. A pitcher of water stood on it and in one corner was an old leather bucket. The chest itself was locked. Alicia moved the pitcher to the floor and sat on the chest. She leaned her head on her hands and tears began to stream down her cheeks.

Hours must have passed—Alicia lost all sense of time. Then at last she heard the sound of the key being turned in the lock of the door. She tensed herself but stayed where she was. It opened, and in came a young woman—and Alicia's heart jumped with joy and amazement. It was Jenny!

She was about to cry out, but Jenny put her finger to her lips in warning, shaking her head to advise her to remain silent until the door closed behind her. Only then did she speak, and it was in a whisper.

'My lady—'

She ran forward with her arms outstretched, and Alicia sprang to her feet and rushed to greet her old friend. They clasped their arms tightly round each other and kissed, and Alicia thought Jenny would squeeze the breath out of her.

'Oh, it is so good to see you,' she whispered.

'Shhh.'

There was the sound of heavy footsteps on the stairs and the two young women sprang apart. Again the door creaked open and two men came in, carrying a mattress and some blankets. Jenny told them to put it down by the wall and, as they left, she spoke to the gaoler.

'I'll just make up the bed for the lady—'

'Let her make up her own—I would,' the gaoler grunted. He put an arm round Jenny's waist and drew her towards him. 'Pretty girl like you shouldn't be bothering your head about looking after another woman—you need a man—'

'Maybe I do—and maybe I don't,' Jenny flirted with him.

'Give us a kiss—'

'Oh, get along with you.' Jenny gave him a push towards the door. 'I'll see you when I've done in here.'

She used a tone of light banter, despite which she kept the gaoler moving back towards the door; as soon as he was through, she slammed it shut.

'Phew! It's lucky he's taken a fancy to me, otherwise I'd never have got in to see you.'

Again Jenny and Alicia flew back into each other's arms and embraced.

'Oh, my lady—it grieves me sorely to see you here like this.'

'It does my heart good just to see you, Jenny.'

'If only I could do something to help you, but the guards have strict instructions to guard you closely.'

'Oh, my dear Jenny, I've wondered so much about what happened at Leet after we left. Was it very terrible for you?'

'There wasn't any more fighting. Captain de Warante called everyone together in the great hall the morning after you left and explained how it had been necessary for Sir Richard to get away and ride as fast as he could to bring back help. We were all terrified for you, but the Captain said he was sure you'd been successful in getting away. He said that if Sir Richard had been captured, there would have been a declaration or something from the enemy. We all cheered when we heard that. Oh, my lady— I was so worried for you.'

'Do go on, please—what happened then?'

'Well, we just stayed quiet, waiting until the lookouts saw the men at arms getting ready to attack. It must have been almost mid-morning, but the Captain said there was no point in letting them know we were giving up until we really had to.

'It was all over very quickly in the end. Captain de Warante rode out and met Rufus Blount and Sir Hobart. He spoke with them and handed over his sword in surrender, but their quarrel was not with de Warante. They had no wish even to take him prisoner. He was allowed to muster his men and leave as soon as Rufus and Sir Hobart entered the castle. They held a court almost immediately and made the tenants pay some rent money and then they were sent back to their farms.'

'It's good to know there was no more blood spilled,' said Alicia. 'And Sir Richard has every hope that with the help of the king he will be able to reclaim Leet. But what of you, Jenny, and Reuben? How did you escape?'

'The castle was occupied and we servants just had to look after the new lot of owners. I'd have put poison in the food, if I'd had my way, and just about everyone felt the same, but they'd have slit our throats if we'd given them the slightest bit of trouble, so there was nothing we could do.'

'You were quite right. Sir Richard knew it would be pointless to fight on in the face of such odds.'

'Anyway, a day or so later, your uncle and Sir Hobart set out to ride to London. I'd overheard a bit of what was going on when I was serving at table—'

'Oh, Jenny—didn't they recognise you?'

'Nay! They can't tell one servant from another. Besides, I'd got different clothes and I made sure my bonnet hung well forward to hide my face.'

Alicia hugged the maid again and Jenny continued her story.

'I soon realised that they knew you'd gone off with Sir Richard and they were determined to get you back. I guessed they wouldn't be too pleased with you and I thought you might need me, so I talked it over with Reuben and we decided to come along here to look for you.'

'Reuben is here too? That's wonderful.'

Jenny gave a little smile. 'Well, he said he couldn't let me come to London on my own—and I was determined—so he had to—Reuben and I like to be together.'

Alicia could well understand that Jenny had been more enthusiastic than Reuben, nevertheless she was grateful to them both.

'You didn't have any difficulty in getting away?'

'No one bothered about us. We got a lift on a carrier's cart for part of the way and the rest of it we walked. We'd only just got here when I saw those ruffians come with that cart and I had a funny feeling about them. It was as though something told me they were up to no good, so I kept watching them. I nearly cried out in horror when I saw them carry you in, my lady. I thought you were dead!'

She paused dramatically, her eyes filling with tears at the thought. Alicia hugged her again.

'Thank goodness you were there.'

'I was there all right. And I crept round and managed to hide behind a door and I heard you speak. Praise be to God! You can't believe how relieved I was.'

'Dear Jenny. What would I do without you? But how did you know to come here?'

'One of the cooks here is Reuben's mother's sister. He said as how we should come here because we might get word about you. He said this house used to belong to your father—did you know that, mistress?'

'I didn't until today, Jenny.'

'He'd turn in his grave if he knew what was going on here. But, my lady—what are we going to do? It breaks my heart to see you held in this dreadful place, a prisoner in what should be your own home. That brute—' they had been talking quietly, but she lowered her voice still further, 'said you were to have nothing to eat or drink, no comforts of any sort, but I wouldn't stand for that. I had to bribe the gaoler, just to let me in—and even money wasn't enough, I had to pretend I actually liked him. Pah!' She spat in disgust.

'I'm sorry I've caused you so much trouble, Jenny—'

'Oh, mistress—I don't mean that. Bless you, it's nothing as long as I managed to get round him. I've brought you some bread and cheese.'

She handed the food to Alicia wrapped in a piece of clean linen.

'Thank you, Jenny. I'll eat it later.'

'Why have they locked you in here, my lady? Are they punishing you for running away?'

'They're trying to force me into that abominable marriage with Sir Hobart. But I can't do it, Jenny, even if I would. I am already married to Sir Richard Calder.'

Jenny's eyes opened wide. She clapped her hands together, so surprised she could hardly believe she had heard aright.

'Oh, my lady! But when? Where?—'

'Only yesterday—or was it the day before. I've lost all sense of time since I've been here. But we were married, truly we were, at the door of one of the churches, I know not which.'

'But where is Sir Richard? Does he know where you are?'

'I think not. I was captured as I walked in the street. Jenny—do you think you could get a message to Sir Richard?'

'That I can and will. Don't you worry, my lady. I'll see to it that he hears about this and he'll be along straight away, I shouldn't wonder, to take you back with him.'

'I hope so—oh, I do hope so.'

'I must go, my lady. The guard'll wonder why I tarry so long. I'll try and come to you again, as soon as I can.'

Moments later Alicia was alone again, but now she did not feel quite so lost, for she had hope. Jenny had braved so much for her already, she would not let her down now. She would certainly take a message to Richard, if it was at all possible. But what then? Would Richard be able to do anything to release her? Would he care enough to try? He had the marriage certificate that would prove his legal right to all her property, so perhaps he would not care what befell his wife.

Alicia slept fitfully. The blankets were hardly sufficient to keep her warm and the chill struck deep into her bones in that dank cellar. In the pitch dark of night it seemed haunted with the ghosts of other prisoners who had been incarcerated there. In her state of near-hysteria she seemed to hear whisperings, moans, to imagine soft damp fingers clawing at her face. Time and again she woke in panic, gazed round in terror, but the black darkness remained impenetrable. Never had a night been so long, but at last dawn broke with a thin shaft of grey light that filtered through the small barred window. There was a relief in having survived, but even in full daylight it remained a gloomy place.

Slowly the hours passed. Alicia had no means of knowing how they went by. She spent some time pacing up and down, and then, for what seemed like hours on end, she just lay on the mattress, covered by the blankets, staring at the brick arch of the roof of her prison. She wished that Jenny would come back, but the door remained locked until late in the afternoon.

Hearing the key turn Alicia sprang up from the mattress and turned eagerly towards the door. Her heart sank when she saw it was her uncle who walked in. The scowl on his face told her he was not come on any kindly errand. She made the obligatory curtsy, though her thoughts were black towards him.

'Well, wench, have you come to your senses?'

'I have never left my senses, my lord, my uncle,' she replied.

'I haven't come here to play silly word-games. You know full well what I mean. I've come for your answer.'

'I have nothing more to say.'

'You're a fool. You realise you will not leave here until you consent to marry Sir Hobart Kimball?'

To that she made no reply.

'You will marry him, you slut,' he hissed the words between teeth clenched with rage.

Despite his fury, Alicia held her head high and stared back at him defiantly.

'So—you defy me still.'

'I will not—I cannot—marry Sir Hobart.'

'Then you'll stay here until you rot. You'll have no food until you agree. 'Twill not be long, I reckon, before you'll lose this stubborn defiance. It takes a full stomach to rebel.'

'My lord, it is as I have told you. I am unable to accede to your request, even if I would, because I am married to Sir Richard Calder.'

'You persist in that cant? I've told you—and the priest agrees with me—that was no marriage, since it had not been consummated.'

'I made my vows, and so did my husband—Sir Richard Calder.'

'Ha! Then I was right. You may have made your vows—but has he yet taken you to bed? You answer me that, wench. It is no marriage until it has been consummated, that's what the law says.'

Perhaps it was as Rufus Blount said. She didn't understand all the legalities that constituted marriage, and he was so insistent on this point that she began to wonder if there was some basis of truth in it. But she had no intention of weakening her position by showing doubt, so she took recourse in repeating again:

'It was a true marriage, sire.'

'How could it have been, when it was made without my consent? That's another point you and that scoundrel Calder overlooked. You are my ward. You were not free to marry whom you pleased, so that union cannot be legal and binding in any way. No court in the land would claim it so.'

'But it is, sire. It is.'

'I see you have not yet found humility.'

He took the whip from his belt, and fearfully she backed away from him. He flicked it towards her so that it made a sharp crack that seemed to fill the cellar with angry sound. The tip of the leather cut against her arm and she cowered away from him, turning her back, instinctively shielding her face. Twice more the whip snaked viciously towards her.

'Think carefully on your situation, wench. Admit you were lying about this so-called marriage.'

'Never.'

'I'll come again tomorrow—and I won't be so patient then. You can have no hope of winning over this. Another twenty-four hours in this place, with nothing to eat, should make you change your mind. If not, I'll have to use stronger measures. Of one thing you can be sure—I'll not be thwarted by a wench, especially by my own niece.'

She remained silent, kept her face turned away from him. She heard him take a step nearer and waited for a further rain of blows, but they did not come. Perhaps even he hesitated to mark her when he hoped soon to be presenting her as a bride.

'All right, my lady. Until tomorrow—and by Christ you'd better have a different answer for me then. I reckon it'll not be long before you're too weak to resist.' He raised his voice and shouted to the guard. 'Open the door.'

Without another word, he left. Alicia was relieved to see him go and yet, strangely, he had brought her a glimmer of hope. Despite her uncle's blustering it was evident that Sir Hobart was still reluctant to proceed with forcing the marriage without her actual consent. She knew it was not simply because she was refusing to say 'yes'; they would have had no qualms in dispensing with that, and would have forged her signature had they believed they could get away with it. It was because Sir Hobart was uncertain whether or not Sir Richard might indeed be able to prove that he had the prior claim to Alicia and her wealth—that was the only reason for their hesitation.

For a moment the relief Alicia felt that Rufus had departed without inflicting any more hurt on her was so great that her spirits lifted, but before long despair returned. Time dragged on its weary way again and, as it passed, hope faded. Her uncle had talked of keeping her here until she died, and she had no doubt he could. He would as soon have her dead as married to Sir Richard.

Hope plummeted still further as the day darkened to night. A whole day without any visit, any word, from Jenny. Had she managed to get word to Richard? If only her faithful maid would come—nothing would keep Jenny away if she could possibly come to her, she was sure of that. What could have happened?

Alicia had only the water in the pitcher to drink, and that tasted stale, unpalatable, so she took just enough to moisten her mouth. She had eaten the bread and cheese long ago and hunger pains gnawed at her stomach. Cold and discomfort added to her agony of mind and made it impossible to sleep. That night seemed even longer than the previous one.

Doubts and uncertainties took root in her mind in those interminable hours of darkness and they grew as the next day progressed, and still no one came. There were so many things that could have gone wrong. Jenny might have been caught and prevented from delivering her message. If that was so, Richard would not know where she was, even yet. Or he might have received the message and been powerless to do anything to free her. Perhaps—and this thought was the hardest of all to bear—perhaps he did not care enough even to try. Their marriage had given him her properties and lands; they would remain his now, even if she died, here in this dank cellar—unless her uncle was right and he could prove that it was not a valid marriage after all. Was that another reason why Richard would do nothing? Anyway, even if he wished to help her, how could he? He had already been driven from Leet Castle by Sir Hobart's men in alliance with those of Rufus Blount—they had outnumbered Richard's force so overwhelmingly— why should she imagine that he would have the power to defeat them here?

Was the only way out to agree to the marriage to Sir Hobart, bigamous though it might be? She could never consent to that while she had her senses—she would rather die! But how horrible to die here, in this dank miserable cellar. Would she have the strength to continue to resist—already she began to feel faint with hunger. The room swam dizzily around her and she stumbled across to the mattress. She lay there, awaiting the threatened visit from her uncle, and still determined never to weaken in her resolve.

CHAPTER
TEN

THE SOUND of the door opening crashed into her half-numbed brain. The grey light that filtered through the small and heavily barred window gave no indication of the time of day. Alicia had long ago lost all sense of time. In her solitary half-starved state she lay crouched on the mattress, with her knees drawn up close, foetus-shaped, needing comfort until at last she had drifted into a fitful sleep.

Someone was coming. Her eyelids fluttered open and she lifted her head. Her spirit, not yet conquered and crushed, told her she must get up. If this was her uncle coming to try once more to persuade her to agree to the horror of marriage with Sir Hobart, then she had to meet him with defiance. If she showed the slightest sign of weakening, he would seize on that and increase the pressure—he would show no mercy. With difficulty, stiff with cold, debilitated by lack of food and drink, she scrambled to her feet. Her knees felt wobbly, she grasped a hook in the wall for support, but she was upright and bravely facing the door when it opened.

'Alicia!'

It was Richard. In two strides he was over to her and had caught her in his arms.

'My lord, my husband,' she murmured.

She clung to him, wondering if it was but a

dream, if he had appeared simply as a product of her disordered mind. She stretched out a hand and touched his handsome face and it felt warm and firm, his chin a little bristly.

'Is—is it really you?'

'It most certainly is—thank God I've found you. Are you all right?'

'Yes—oh, Richard—'

Tears of relief and pent-up emotion were running down her cheeks. She wiped them away impatiently.

'I'm sorry—I'm all right really—'

'Can you walk?'

'I—I think so—' Then, as the realisation of this joy fully reacted in her mind like a burst of brilliant sunshine, she exclaimed, 'Oh, yes—I can certainly walk, if it be away from this hateful place!'

Even as she spoke and began to take a step forward, she stumbled and would have fallen, but Richard put an arm around her and its strength was steadying.

'I'll carry you.'

He picked her up as easily as if she were a child and climbed the stone steps that led from her prison to those beautiful rooms above. They were filled with sunshine and light, which surprised her after the dimness below. Gently he set her down on a bench, close to that window with the heraldic arms of her family worked into it in stained glass. She saw now that it opened to lawns and formal gardens outside.

Jenny was there, and she rushed towards Alicia and bent in a deep curtsy, yet clasped her mistress's hand and kissed it as she did so. Alicia smiled and bade her rise, and Jenny was all smiles and happiness and also concern for her mistress's well-being.

'Oh, my lady—forgive me for not coming to you yesterday. I took the message to Sir Richard, but then I was unable to get back into the house, everywhere was close locked and even Reuben couldn't let me in because of the guards, and so I couldn't come to you.'

' 'Tis no matter, Jenny. You have done the important thing and secured my release.'

'Oh, it's so good to see you here, where you belong, my lady. But I mustn't stand here chattering—you must be starving. I'll fetch you some food straight away.'

Alicia looked around, still with a sense of wonder and disbelief.

'Where is my uncle—and Sir Hobart?'

Richard gave a harsh laugh. 'You won't be troubled by them again, Alicia. They've been taken to the Fleet Prison.'

Her heart leapt—it was impossible not to feel relieved at that news.

'Oh, Richard—they—they tried to force me—into a marriage—'

'I know. Don't distress yourself by thinking of it, Alicia. That's all over and they'll be punished for their presumption.'

'But how—'

He sat down beside her on the bench and leaned back, looking well pleased with himself, then began to explain.

'I had already secured an audience with the king and told His Majesty how those blackguards had illegally captured Leet Castle, and the king recognised the rightness of my case. But when I returned to my house, you were missing, Alicia. The ser-

vants told me you'd gone to the cloth mercer with
Ellen but that neither of you had returned. I was
furious that they had allowed you out without an
escort—I sent servants everywhere I could think of
to search for you—'

'But Ellen? What of her?'

'She's back now—and safe. But it was only when
Jenny came to me and told me where to find you
that I was able to act. The king had already promised men to accompany me to Leet to regain my
possessions, and I mustered them as speedily as
possible and came here. They were the king's men
and it would have been treason if those villians had
not surrendered, so there was little trouble.'

'God be praised! What will happen to them?'

'That remains to be seen. They are to be brought
before the court and charged, not only with taking
Leet by force, but also with trying to defraud me of
the properties you brought me on your marriage.'

Until that moment, when Sir Richard spoke so
coolly of her properties, she had cherished a small,
faint hope that, despite all the evidence she had
heard, he had not known of her inheritance. She
had almost pushed such a dream from her con-
sciousness, but it had refused quite to die, because
she had so very much wanted to believe that there
had been love—that Richard's motive in marrying
her had not been wholly mercenary. Now he was
trampling that cherished hope like a delicate bud
beneath his heel.

'You—you knew about my inheritance?'

'Of course, as soon as you told me your name, for
it was well known in court circles that Rufus Blount
was seeking a match for you that would be advantageous to himself.'

It seemed that everyone had known, except herself. Alicia heaved a sigh. What a naive country wench she must have seemed.

'Even after we'd captured your uncle he tried to bluster his way out of it, tried to tell me that we were not truly married because he hadn't given his consent. He knows he's got nothing to gain from your marriage to me.'

Richard laughed in sheer delight that he had outwitted Sir Hobart and her uncle at their own game in the matrimonial stakes. He made no attempt to soften the truth. He had known all along that she had lands and houses, that this town house and Braister Castle and those other manors were hers by right. Why should he care about her feelings now? He had won, and the light of victory shone in his face, danced in his eyes, came from his throat in a chuckle of delight.

Alicia bent her head; she couldn't bear to look at him in this mood. What a fool she had been to cherish that fantasy of a marriage for love! Life was not like that. Such things happened only in stories and ballads. Sir Richard Calder was no different from other men. He had married her not for herself, not from love or tenderness or even pity, but just to acquire her property.

She tried not to show her deep disappointment. After all, being Richard's wife must be infinitely better than being married to Sir Hobart. It was that woman Elizabeth Woodville whom Richard was in love with. That had been plain from the moment she had arrived at Leet—but would this intense jealousy remain with her for ever? If she had been married to Sir Hobart she would have welcomed it if he had taken a mistress, for she was sure she would never have overcome her repugnance at the thought of being made love to by him. With Richard she knew that his love-making could awaken a fire of erotic excitement in her—but that very ecstasy would make his unfaithfulness all the harder to bear.

She would try to be submissive, uncomplaining—perhaps if she bore him a son he might begin to feel some tenderness towards her. That at least was a hope to latch on to. Then Jenny came back, carrying a tray on which was a steaming bowl of soup made of meat and vegetables and herbs, and the aroma that rose from it was so delicious that Alicia's mouth watered. She also brought bread, butter, cheese, jams, pickles and ale.

'The larder is well stocked, my lady. The housekeeper here knows her business,' Jenny said approvingly. 'I've brought these, but if there's anything other you wish for—'

'I'm sure this is more than adequate,' Alicia smiled.

She was ravenously hungry and began to eat at once, while Jenny stood by, nodding her head with satisfaction, as if she saw her mistress gaining strength with every mouthful.

'Take care of your lady well, Jenny,' said Sir Richard. 'See that she eats and rests. I would be glad to see a touch of colour in her cheeks by the time I return.'

'Yes, my lord.' Jenny bobbed a curtsy.

Richard turned to Alicia. 'This evening I wish to take you to visit some good friends of mine.'

She looked up at him in surprise.

'Oh, dear—must I? I— don't know—'

'It is important,' he said brusquely.

'But who—?'

'I can tell you no more at the moment,' he interrupted. 'But see that you are looking as well as you can and be ready by the hour of seven.'

'Yes, my lord.'

'Good. I've some matters to attend to meanwhile.'

With the briefest of bows he left the room. Alicia stared after his departing figure and heaved a sigh. His abrupt manner seemed to have taken away all her appetite, but Jenny, watching her keenly, would have none of that.

'Now, my lady—finish up that bowl of soup and then just try a little of this cold salt beef. I vow you'll say you never tasted better.'

Alicia did as she was bidden, knowing Jenny was trying to raise her spirits. She took a mouthful— and it was indeed delicious—and her youthful healthy hunger came back, reminding her she had been starved for two days. When she had eaten her fill, in came Ellen, her arms piled high with the finished gowns that had been ordered on the day Alicia was abducted by Rufus and Sir Hobart.

'Ellen!' Alicia was delighted to see the girl again. 'You escaped!'

'My lady.' Ellen curtsyed. She gave a light chuckle. 'They didn't know London as I do. I soon gave those ruffians the slip—dodged down an alleyway, through a yard and into a swordsmith's workshop. The owner and his apprentices are old friends of mine. I hid there until I was sure they'd given up looking for me, then I went back to my lord Calder's house and told him what had happened.'

She paused, then added ruefully, 'I thought my lord would have murdered me for letting them take you, my lady—but praise be to God he understood that there was nothing I could do. Then Jenny came, and it was wonderful, for she told my lord just where to find you. Oh, my lady—I feared for your life and I'm so happy that you're back with us again.'

It was warming to have two such good servants whom Alicia could also think of as friends. Both were so anxious to please, each even a little jealous of the administrations of the other. When Jenny had satisfied herself that Alicia had eaten as much as she possibly could, she tried to persuade her mistress to retire to her bed-chamber and sleep.

'I would prefer to rest in the garden, as it's such a lovely day,' Alicia said. 'I've been shut away from the sunshine and fresh air for two long days or more.'

'I'll show you the bower, my lady,' said Ellen.

She led Alicia to the far end of the garden where there was a seat and a trellis covered with roses. From there she could look back across the neatly tended garden beds to the fine red-brick house, and the thought that there would be many times when she would be able to sit there in the years to come gave her a curiously sad pleasure. How much more pleasant it would have been had Richard been beside her. Where was he now? Had he again gone to visit Elizabeth Woodville? She closed her eyes and made an effort to erase that picture from her mind. Soon she dozed off and slept lightly for an hour or so, watched over by Jenny and Ellen. Then it was time to repair to the bed-chamber, and both maids insisted on helping Alicia with her toilette.

'I wonder where my lord wishes to escort me?' Alicia mused aloud.

'I have no idea, my lady. My instructions were to see that you were elegantly attired for a formal occasion.'

Together Jenny and Ellen assisted Alicia into the new shift. It was made of the softest silk with an embroidered top which was revealed by the fashionably deep cut vee of the upper gown. This was dusky pink with a tightly-fitting bodice which clung to her figure. It had been worked with great skill, the skirt full and gathered and decorated with a wealth of appliqué and other needlework, and so long that it trailed on the floor behind her. Alicia had never before possessed such a beautiful gown and she marvelled that it could have been made so speedily.

There was still a heady joy in being free, in knowing that the threat of marriage to Sir Hobart had been thrust away for ever. Moreover the rest and the food had given her strength and courage. Her confidence began to return as she donned the new clothes that replaced the borrowed gown in which she had lived day and night since she had been imprisoned.

Yet still her pleasure was tempered by the knowledge that her husband would never feel the depth of love for her that he did for the beautiful Elizabeth Woodville. For that lady he had even left her on their wedding night. That desertion she was sure she would never forgive or forget, it made her much more miserable than the realisation that Richard had married her for her fortune. She tried to feel humbly grateful—after all it could so easily have been the hated Sir Hobart Kimball that she now awaited, but there was little of joy or romance in her heart as she prepared for her first entry into London society as Lady Alicia Calder.

Almost as soon as she was ready there was a knock on the door and Sir Richard entered the room. He looked her over as if her appearance was of great moment to him, but on this occasion it was with no fire of desire, simply with a cool critical appreciation. There was even something in that look that reminded her uncomfortably of the way in which Aunt Margaret had eyed her before taking her down to be presented to Sir Hobart that evening that seemed so long ago, making her feel as if she was a commodity, not a person.

Jenny and Ellen stood to one side, waiting anxiously for their lord's assessment. Alicia lifted her head and stared back at him with a look of proud disdain. If he wished their relationship to be cool—then that was how she would let it be.

'Good,' he commented at last.

He held out a hand, which obviously indicated that she should place hers in its grasp and accompany him. This she did, keeping her head held high, while Jenny bustled along behind her, lifting her mistress's long trailing skirts.

They walked out to the courtyard where horses awaited them. A pretty mare was harnessed with a side-saddle. Jenny tucked up one side of Alicia's skirts and, assisted by Richard, Alicia mounted and perched herself there while the maid decorously adjusted the yards of material that made up her gown. With such an elaborate skirt to be attended to, not to mention the high steeple headdress, riding was by no means easy. Alicia found herself chafing at the inconvenience of it.

Richard rode beside her as, accompanied by
Jenny and two men-servants on foot, they walked
their horses out of the courtyard and turned into
the street where pedestrians moved out of their
way. The journey took them along West Cheap and
past St Paul's Cathedral, a building in early English
Gothic style with a spire almost five hundred feet
high. They passed through Ludgate and as she
caught sight of the Fleet Prison Alicia shuddered to
think that her uncle Rufus and Sir Hobart were
held there awaiting trial. The horses' hooves clattered as they crossed the bridge over the Fleet
stream and carried on along Fleet Street.

Alicia would have been fascinated by all that she
saw, except that everything seemed to be coloured
by a flat greyness that she knew was caused by her
own lack of spirits. The joy she had experienced
when last she had threaded her way with Richard
through the streets of London to plight their
troth—that had left her. Love had been blanketed
by the reality of business.

'Where are we going, my lord?' she ventured to
ask.

'To Westminster Palace, to present you to the
king and—' he lowered his voice so that only she
could hear—'to the queen.'

Alicia gasped. That was something she had never
anticipated. She knew that Richard had sought and
received his sovereign's aid in solving his difficulties—yet she had never even imagined that she
might be presented at court. Another query sprang
into her mind.

'Did you say—' she began, then remembering
with what caution he had spoken, she whispered as
she finished,—'the queen?'

'That is so,' he replied evenly.

'I hadn't heard the king had taken a wife.'

'It isn't generally known—and it's going to surprise a lot of people when it does come out.'

'You mean he's married in secret?'

'Exactly.'

'But why?'

'Mainly because of Warwick, who thinks the only possible wife for our good King Edward of England would be a foreign princess. He schemes and plots to that end, even now he's in France where he's been trying to arrange a match with Princess Bona of Savoy.'

Richard found this highly amusing. He paused to chuckle over the news. Then, riding very close to Alicia so that only she could hear, he continued.

'The king was in fact married several weeks ago. I was one of the few people to have been taken into his confidence. He fell in love with an Englishwoman, who is not even of royal blood—moreover, she is a widow, with two small sons both below the age of five. Now at last the king has decided to make the news of his marriage public and, thank goodness, the need for secrecy is over. But it was a matter on which I was able to give the king some service.'

'That's why he's been so helpful to you?'

'In part—but we've been friends from boyhood, as I told you. I'm anxious that you should meet their majesties without delay. The country is still full of dangers. We have bested Blount and Kimball for the moment, but this dreadful civil war that men so romantically call the War of the Roses is not yet over. We know not what the future may bring, Alicia, and should any ill ever befall me—then you will have need of influential friends.'

'I pray that may never be necessary, my lord,' Alicia said fervently.

'Amen to that. I have no intention of courting danger, but soon I shall ride forth to retake Leet and I shall go more happily if I know that the king is your friend as well as mine. So you will see why I felt the matter to be urgent.'

'Yes, my lord. I shall do my best to make a good impression.'

How very practical he was. Somehow that was a side of his nature that Alicia had not noticed before, another matter to which she had to reconcile herself. Things were not proceeding at all as she had anticipated. She took little heed of where Richard was leading her until they entered the courtyard of Westminster Palace.

There was an air of unreality in the splendour of the building, in the uniform of the guards, in the elegance of the trappings and the very size of the place, before they were ushered into the presence of King Edward IV. He was not seated on a throne, as Alicia in her naivety had expected, but on a chair, a comfortable ordinary chair close to a magnificent window.

Even though he was seated she could tell that he was a tall man with broad shoulders, and had she not known Richard she might have agreed with the chronicler who said King Edward was 'the handsomest young knight in all England'. He was exquisitely attired, his black velvet cap decorated with a large fleur-de-lis of precious stones and he wore a tunic of cloth of gold.

As was becoming in a humble subject, Alicia

made this appraisal of her monarch quickly—then
her gaze turned to the lady at his side—and her
footsteps faltered. She almost stopped moving forward, probably would have halted completely, had
not her hand been tucked firmly into Richard's
arm. She knew the lady at once. It was Elizabeth
Woodville.

Sir Richard knelt before his king, and Alicia gave
her very deepest curtsy. As she remained in that
position of humility before her monarch, thoughts
raced round her head in wonderment—could it
really be that Elizabeth Woodville was the queen of
England?

'Rise,' commanded the king.

Then at once the atmosphere was more relaxed.

'Lady Alicia,' said the king. 'I have listened to
your name on the lips of my good and loyal subject,
Sir Richard Calder, more often than I care to
mention. You have a fine man for your husband.
Queen Elizabeth and I wish you both a long,
happy, and prosperous life.'

'Thank you, your majesty,' Alicia murmured.

She felt quite tongue-tied in the royal presence
and found herself staring rather more than was
polite at the young king and his beautiful wife.
Suddenly the queen smiled at her.

'You are astonished to see me here? That is
proof—if any further proof were needed, of the
trustworthiness of my lord Calder, for I recollect
that you and I met at Leet Castle just before it was
attacked.'

'That is true,' murmured Alicia.

'It would have been disastrous not only for me,
but also for the king, if I had fallen into the hands of
those scoundrels. So I owe a debt of gratitude both

to Sir Richard and to you for the timely warning
you brought.'

'I am glad to have been of some small service,'
was all Alicia could say.

Her mind was in a turmoil. She was overjoyed to
discover that Elizabeth was not Richard's mistress
and could hardly believe it was true, even now,
when she was in the presence of their majesties.
Yet it was plain for her to see—there was no
mistaking the look of adoration that was on the face
of the handsome young king every time he looked
at Elizabeth. How wonderful it must be to be so
loved!

Elizabeth was a beautiful young woman, dressed
in a rather sober fashion, with her hair drawn back
severely and covered by a small embroidered close-
fitting cap, yet she had a charming smile and a ready
turn of wit that helped to put Alicia at her ease. She
leaned towards her confidentially.

'I must tell you what a wonderful friend Sir
Richard has been. Only the other evening a message came to me from a good friend I have in the
French court and I learned that that bully, Warwick, was about to announce an engagement between my dear husband and the French princess,
the one they call Princess Bona, sister of the
queen.'

'Oh, your majesty—how dreadful for you,' exclaimed Alicia.

'Exactly. You can imagine I was quite distraught,
and I didn't know to whom I could turn, because
Edward was out of town and I had to find someone I
could trust absolutely as a go-between. I dared not
send even a written message for fear of it falling
into the wrong hands. So I sent for Sir Richard and

he came at once. You'll never know how much that meant to me—for not only did he take the message but, because of its import, he persuaded Edward that the time for secrecy must be over.'

So that was the reason Richard had left so abruptly on their wedding night! It took all Alicia's strength of mind to retain her composure.

'You must be glad now that you can take your rightful place as queen, your majesty,' she managed to say.

'Yes. You're right, of course, my dear—and yet—' the queen paused and her eyes grew a little wistful. 'I shall always be grateful that we had those few months to live our idyll, when we were free to be lovers without the cares of state and its pomp and circumstance formalising it all.'

At last so much was made plain. Of course Richard had to send men to escort the queen safely to London, even though it made his castle at Leet impossible to defend. Now too she knew why he had deserted her on their wedding night—that command from the queen could certainly not be ignored. Alicia lowered her head, ashamed of the jealous thoughts she had harboured. Indeed, it suddenly occurred to her, her suspicions were probably treasonable!

'Now, tell me about yourself,' asked the queen. 'Is this your first visit to London?'

'Yes, your majesty.'

'And do you like it here?'

'I—I've hardly seen anything of the city yet,' Alicia murmured.

'Of course—I was forgetting that terrible business about your abduction. I trust you are quite recovered from that misadventure?'

'Yes, thank you, ma'am.'

'Richard tells me you come from Norfolk. I've been there recently, on a pilgrimage to Walsingham. Indeed it was as I was returning from my devotions there that I stayed at Leet, for it was a long and tiring journey.'

For some twenty minutes they chatted in a friendly fashion while the king and Richard discussed the problems that might be encountered in the retaking of Richard's property. To forestall any difficulties, the king dictated a letter to his scribe in which he pledged his full support. It was sealed with the royal seal so that it would be a bold man who would dare to defy such an order, and Richard received it gratefully.

An equerry walked over and spoke to the king. Another pressing engagement awaited him. With the required low obeisances Alicia and Richard bade farewell and retreated from the royal presence. Even before they had left the room another knight was striding into the great hall, seeking audience.

Alicia was longing to ask more about this secret marriage, and would have liked to linger, looking around her at the palace itself, but Richard hurried her away and back to their horses. There was no chance to speak a word to him until they were again mounted and clattering through the shadowy streets, accompanied, as when they set out, by Jenny and the two men-servants.

'Oh, Richard—I—I had no idea who she was when—when I met the queen at Leet,' Alicia said.

He gave a light laugh. 'I dared not tell you the truth, for Elizabeth Woodville had many enemies who would have been only too willing to harm her.'

'I—I can still hardly believe it! King Edward of all people to marry in secret!' Alicia exclaimed. 'My uncle always said he just did what the Earl of Warwick told him.'

'Lots of lies are spread abroad, especially in troubled times such as we live in,' replied Richard. 'Nevertheless it's true there will be many who won't be pleased when it becomes more widely known.'

Alicia recalled the disparaging way in which her uncle and Sir Hobart had spoken of Elizabeth Woodville, and it kindled curiosity in her.

'Does she come of a good family?' she asked.

'She's the daughter of Sir Richard Woodville, who distinguished himself in the French war. Her mother was Jacquetta of Luxembourg, who was previously married to the Duke of Bedford.'

'And Queen Elizabeth has also been married before, hasn't she?'

'At eighteen she was married to Sir John Grey, but he was killed in the second Battle of St Albans.'

Alicia sighed. 'It is such a pity there will now be no great wedding ceremony for the king.'

'You hanker for some excitement, Alicia? I would not have thought you had found life so dull lately?'

'I've never seen a great state occasion of any sort—I would truly like to.'

'Well, I understand that, now the king has de-cided to make his marriage public, there will be a grand coronation so that her majesty may be officially accepted by the nation.'

'Shall we be in London when that takes place?'

'Most certainly. All the loyal knights will be

required to be in attendance on such an occasion—
and there'll be plenty of feasting, dancing and
merriment.'

They rode into the stableyard behind Richard's
house. The groom was there, busily rubbing down a
large horse which, to judge by the lather it was in,
had just travelled at great speed and for a long
distance.

'Richard!'

A familiar deep voice boomed from the gateway
that led to the garden, and there was Brian de
Warante, his arms outstretched in greeting.

'By all that's wonderful! Brian!'

The two men embraced, slapping their hands on
each other's shoulders in joy that was all the greater
because it contained an element of relief.

'You got away safely—I knew you could do it,
Richard! I'm proud of you,' exclaimed de Warante.
'Tell me all that happened.'

'I will indeed,' said Richard.

Alicia stood patiently by Richard's side as he
recounted their adventures, keeping his account as
brief as possible, for he was eager to hear about the
surrender of Leet Castle. Brian explained that he
had taken care that it should happen with the least
possible damage to the building, believing that
before long Richard would be in a position to
retake it.

'But you—what of you, my old friend? They
didn't harm you?' asked Richard.

'Nay. I was of no interest to them. They took me
for a mercenary. I negotiated a safe passage for my
men and for myself and they were willing enough to
grant it. It was in their best interests to take the
castle with as little damage as possible. They con-

tented themselves with disarming us and jeering as they drove us out of the castle on foot.'

'And what did you do then?'

'I stayed close to Leet for a few days, to see for myself what would happen there. Rufus Blount held a Manor Court straight away and he made the tenants pay double their usual dues, whether they could afford it or not. He's a hated man there, I can tell you.'

'That doesn't surprise me, Brian.'

'He and Sir Hobart stayed only a couple of days, then they set out for London. I didn't know whether I would be best able to serve you by following them, or by staying to find out the strength they had left in the castle—and I decided to do that.'

'You did well, my friend. And did they leave a large garrison in possession?'

'Large enough—but I've heard that their men have not been paid and they're muttering against their lord.'

'How do you know this?'

'You still have loyal servants at Leet, both within and without the castle. When you are ready to retake, they will rise up to your assistance.'

'We ride tomorrow,' said Richard.

Alicia felt her heart contract. More fighting— would it never end? Yet she knew, as did every member of every noble family in the land, that to keep property you had to be prepared to fight for it. A movement by Richard broke into her thoughts. He reached out a hand and drew her to his side.

'Brian—there is one other matter of which I have to tell you. This lady is now my wife.'

Slowly, as he recovered from his initial surprise,

a great smile spread over the usually dour face of de
Warante.

'By all that's wonderful, Richard. So you've
decided to marry at last—do you know, I thought
you'd never make up your mind to it. And, by
Christ, you've done well for yourself!'

'Aye. I think so too,' Richard replied tersely.

Brian took a couple of steps towards Alicia and
lifted her hand to his lips.

'My blessing on both of you.'

'I thank you, sir,' she smiled.

Together they walked towards the house but, at
the door, Richard indicated that she should enter
alone.

'My lady,' he said. 'I'll join you within the hour
for the evening meal. Come, Brian—we must consult together on strategy.'

Jenny accompanied her mistress into the great
hall, where once again a fine meal was being prepared by the servants. There was nothing she could
do but sit and wait. She folded her hands into her
lap and adopted a pose of patient resignation. She
had been pleased to see Brian de Warante again,
but was nevertheless dismayed that he and Richard
were yet again preparing to go into battle. She had
known of course, that Richard was planning to set
off to retake Leet, but somehow she hadn't expected it to be so soon. *We ride tomorrow*, he had
said. He was all eagerness to be off now that he had
that letter from King Edward and the troop of men
to lead.

That interview they'd had that afternoon with
the king and his new queen was still in the forefront
of Alicia's mind. What a favoured woman was
Elizabeth. Not only was she the first woman in the

land, queen of England, but Edward had been so much in love with her that he had married her in secret. Such a rash step could have cost him his throne, but he had taken that risk rather than contract the more usual loveless marriage of convenience. It was so romantic—Alicia's eyes misted with tears. How wonderful it would be to be loved like that—by Richard. She forced herself to face the fact that it could never be. She knew now that she had no cause to be jealous of Elizabeth, but would she ever be able to forget that he had married her only for her dowry?

The hour passed slowly but at last Richard came striding into the great hall, and again she noticed that there was a light of excitement in his eyes. She had seen it before, when he had been preparing and taking part in the battle of Leet Castle. He was a fighting man and he had just been making arrangements to lead his troops into battle to regain his possessions. She had no illusions as to why that twinkle of excitement shone in his face, lit his eyes, even made a mocking smile break over his face as he made a courteous bow to her.

'My lady—shall we dine?'

He offered her his arm and gallantly escorted her to the table. He had been followed into the great hall by Brian de Warante, who now took his accustomed place on the left of Sir Richard at the top table. Alicia, in her position of wife, was seated on Sir Richard's right. Ale and wine flowed freely, as if this was a night of celebration, as indeed it was, in thanks for the safe return of Brian de Warante. Alicia noticed that although Richard was obviously in a convivial mood and encouraged those around him to drink freely, he himself remained quite abstemious. She caught from him an aura of excitement and when he looked at her, as he did several times in the course of the meal, she found herself unable to meet the challenge that sparkled in the depths of his dark eyes.

When the time came for the tables to be cleared, Richard, keeping Alicia close beside him, ordered their seats to be placed at the end of the room. It was a warm evening and there was no need to draw up to the fire. Presently the assembled company began to dance merry jigs and to sing together, getting noisier as the evening wore on.

Richard made no attempt to join in the gaiety but Alicia caught a glow of anticipation from him. He was totally male that evening—prepared to ride forth into battle, eager for that confrontation, but eager too for the consummation of their marriage. Each time he looked at her she felt strangely, deliciously, threatened and could only lower her eyes so that they were veiled by her long sweeping lashes. When he lifted her hand to his lips and kissed it, his touch sent a thrill of anticipation through her and she looked up at him with wonderment at this gentleness, and the expression in his eyes left her in no doubt that it was time for her to retire.

After Jenny had withdrawn, Alicia lay in the great bed with the sheets drawn up close to her chin to cover her nakedness. She felt both excited and shy as she awaited her lord, but she had no time to analyse those sensations for he was there almost as soon as Jenny had left the bed-chamber.

She trembled as he approached the bed and stood looking down at her and, although she still held the covers close to her chin, his dark eyes, mysterious pools in the dimly-lit room, seemed almost to devour her. The excitement that had charged the atmosphere around them all evening exploded into passion now that they were at last alone.

Gently he moved her hands aside and lifted the bed-covers. Firelight flickered on her nakedness. He remained still, just gazing down at her, and the expression in his eyes kindled the flame of love in her as tangibly as if it was a physical caress.

'How beautiful you are.'

They were caught in an enveloping rapture—nothing now could keep their bodies apart. Unable to hold himself away from her a moment longer, he seized her close in his arms and his lips claimed hers in a wild, hungry kiss that held her clinging to him as if her mouth had fused into his. He clasped her and kissed her and it seemed he would never let her go. When at last he lifted his face and drew back, his eyes still looked deeply into hers.

'Amandus,' he murmured softly.

It sounded sweetly on his tongue and she smiled gently up at his face that was so close to hers, and remembered that night at the inn when he had given her that unusual name. Strange that he should have used it again now, for he had never spoken it to her since.

'You said it had a special meaning,' she reminded him. 'What is it?'

'*Amandus*.' He said it again, his voice turning the name into a caress. 'It means, my sweet Alicia—it means just what you are—*worthy of love*.'

Her eyes opened wide with wonder. *Worthy of love*. The words sang in her heart with an uprush of joy, for she recollected that he had given her that name even before she had told him who her real parents were, before he could have known of the property she would bring to the man she married. He had christened her *Amandus* when he had believed her to be but a penniless orphan, and her love for him knew no bounds.

'Was it not a well-chosen name?' he asked.

'Oh, my love—I think I must be the most fortunate woman in all London.'

'My dearest—my sweet Alicia—to me you will always be *Amandus*, for I do most truly love you.'

She would have told him too of her love but she had no opportunity, for his mouth again sought hers. Words could scarcely have expressed her feelings any more fervently and beautifully than did the way she twined her arms round him as she abandoned herself to his embrace. She wanted only to belong to him as, with more tender kisses and gentle caresses, he made love to her, arousing in her an all-consuming passion, a fire that would never again be quite extinguished.

The next morning she awoke to find that Richard was stirring at her side.

'My dearest,' he murmured.

'My lord,' she replied, and in her smiling face was a look of such unabashed love that he bent and began kissing her all over again. She lifted her arms and twined them about his neck.

'Sweet Alicia,' he murmured, with his lips still close to her mouth. 'Would that I could stay with you all day long.'

'My lord—that is all my wish too.'

'I have to ride this day to retake possession of Leet.'

'Then, my lord, my husband, I shall ride with you.'

'It would be more seemly for you to reside here in London while I attend to these matters,' he said.

'I care not a jot for what is seemly—you must know that, dearest Richard. My place is at your side—and it is there I intend always to be, unless you positively order me to do otherwise.'

'Cunning wench—sweet Alicia—you know I cannot bring myself to make such an order.'

'Then my lord, dear husband—I shall rise immediately and prepare to ride forth at your side—as I shall be from this day on.'

Mills & Boon

Your chance to step into the past Take 2 Books FREE

Discover a world long vanished. An age of chivalry and intrigue, powerful desires and exotic locations. Read about true love found by soldiers and statesmen, princesses and serving girls. All written as only Mills & Boon's top-selling authors know how. Become a regular reader of Mills & Boon Masquerade Historical Romances and enjoy 4 superb, new titles every two months, plus a whole range of special benefits: your very own personal membership card entitles you to a regular free newsletter packed with recipes, competitions, exclusive book offers plus other bargain offers and big cash savings.

AND an Introductory FREE GIFT for YOU.
Turn over the page for details.

Fill in and send this coupon back today
and we will send you

2 Introductory
Historical Romances
FREE

At the same time we will reserve a subscription to
Mills & Boon Masquerade Historical Romances for
you. Every two months you will receive Four new,
superb titles delivered direct to your door. You
don't pay extra for delivery. Postage and packing is
always completely free. There is no obligation or
commitment – you only receive books for as long as
you want to.

**Just fill in and post the coupon today to MILLS & BOON
READER SERVICE, FREEPOST, P.O. BOX 236, CROYDON,
SURREY CR9 9EL.**

Please Note:- READERS IN SOUTH AFRICA write to
Mills & Boon, Postbag X3010,
Randburg 2125, S. Africa.

FREE BOOKS CERTIFICATE

**To: Mills & Boon Reader Service, FREEPOST, P.O. Box 236,
Croydon, Surrey CR9 9EL.**

Please send me, free and without obligation, two Masquerade Historical Romances, and
reserve a Reader Service Subscription for me. If I decide to subscribe I shall receive,
following my free parcel of books, four new Masquerade Historical Romances every two
months for £5.00, post and packing free. If I decide not to subscribe, I shall write to you
within 10 days. The free books are mine to keep in any case. I understand that I may cancel
my subscription at any time simply by writing to you. I am over 18 years of age.

Please write in BLOCK CAPITALS.

Signature _____

Name _____

Address _____

_____ Post code _____

SEND NO MONEY — TAKE NO RISKS.

Please don't forget to include your Postcode.

Remember, postcodes speed delivery. Offer applies in UK only and is not valid
to present subscribers. Mills & Boon reserve the right to exercise discretion in
granting membership. If price changes are necessary you will be notified.

4M   *Offer expires July 31st 1984.*

EP9M